EMMA McCHESNEY & CO.

Edna Ferber

Illustrated by J. Henry

University of Illinois Press
Urbana and Chicago

First Illinois paperback, 2002

∞ This book is printed on acid-free paper.

Library of Congress Cataloging-in-Publication Data
Ferber, Emma, 1887-1968.
Emma McChesney & Co. / Edna Ferber ;
illustrations by J. Henry.
p. cm.
ISBN 0-252-07088-7 (alk. paper)
1. McChesney, Emma (Fictitious character)—
Fiction. 2. Traveling sales personnel—Fiction.
3. Women sales personnel—Fiction.
4. Businesswomen—Fiction. I. Title.
PS3511.E46E53   2002
813'.52—dc21   2002017119

EMMA McCHESNEY & CO.

"There passed from her white fingers to his brown ones that
which is the Esperanto of the nations"—*Page 30*

CONTENTS

ILLUSTRATIONS

EMMA McCHESNEY & CO.

I

BROADWAY TO BUENOS AIRES

THE door marked "MRS. MCCHESNEY" was closed. T. A. Buck, president of the Buck Featherloom Petticoat Company, coming gaily down the hall, stopped before it, dismayed, as one who, with a spicy bit of news at his tongue's end, is met with rebuff before the first syllable is voiced. That closed door meant: "Busy. Keep out."

"She'll be reading a letter," T. A. Buck told himself grimly. Then he turned the knob and entered his partner's office.

Mrs. Emma McChesney was reading a letter. More than that, she was poring over it so that, at the interruption, she glanced up in a maddeningly half-cocked manner which conveyed the impression that, while her physical eye beheld the intruder, her mental eye was still on the letter.

"I knew it," said T. A. Buck morosely.

Emma McChesney put down the letter and smiled.

"Sit down—now that you're in. And if you expect me to say, 'Knew what?' you're doomed to disappointment."

T. A. Buck remained standing, both gloved hands clasping his walking stick on which he leaned.

"Every time I come into this office, you're reading the latest scrawl from your son. One would think Jock's letters were deathless masterpieces. I believe you read them at half-hour intervals all week, and on Sunday get 'em all out and play solitaire with them."

Emma McChesney's smile widened frankly to a grin.

"You make me feel like a cash-girl who's been caught flirting with the elevator starter. Have I been neglecting business?"

"Business? No; you've been neglecting me!"

"Now, T. A., you've just come from the tailor's, and I suppose it didn't fit in the back."

"It isn't that," interrupted Buck, "and you

know it. Look here! That day Jock went away and we came back to the office, and you said——"

"I know I said it, T. A., but don't remind me of it. That wasn't a fair test. I had just seen Jock leave me to take his own place in the world. You know that my day began and ended with him. He was my reason for everything. When I saw him off for Chicago that day, and knew he was going there to stay, it seemed a million miles from New York. I was blue and lonely and heart-sick. If the office-boy had thrown a kind word to me I'd have broken down and wept on his shoulder."

Buck, still standing, looked down between narrowed lids at his business partner.

"Emma McChesney," he said steadily, "do you mean that?"

Mrs. McChesney, the straightforward, looked up, looked down, fiddled with the letter in her hand.

"Well—practically yes—that is—I thought, now that you're going to the mountains for a month, it might give me a chance to think— to——"

"And d'you know what I'll do meanwhile,

[3]

out of revenge on the sex? I've just ordered three suits of white flannel, and I shall break every feminine heart in the camp, regardless— Oh, say, that's what I came in to tell you! Guess whom I saw at the tailor's?"

"Well, Mr. Bones, whom did you, and so forth?"

"Fat Ed Meyers. I just glimpsed him in one of the fitting-rooms. And they were draping him in white."

Emma McChesney sat up with a jerk.

"Are you sure?"

"Sure? There's only one figure like that. He had the thing on and was surveying himself in the mirror—or as much of himself as could be seen in one ordinary mirror. In that white suit, with his red face above it, he looked like those pictures you see labeled, 'Sunrise on Snow-covered Mountain.'"

"Did he see——"

"He dodged when he saw me. Actually! At least, he seems to have the decency to be ashamed of the deal he gave us when he left us flat in the thick of his Middle Western trip and went back to the Sans-Silk Skirt Company. I wanted him to know I had seen him. As

I passed, I said, 'You'll mow 'em down in those clothes, Meyers.' " Buck sat down in his leisurely fashion, and laughed his low, pleasant laugh. "Can't you see him, Emma, at the seashore?"

But something in Emma McChesney's eyes, and something in her set, unsmiling face, told him that she was not seeing seashores. She was staring straight at him, straight through him, miles beyond him. There was about her that tense, electric, breathless air of complete detachment, which always enveloped her when her lightning mind was leaping ahead to a goal unguessed by the slower thinking.

"What's your tailor's name?"

"Name? Trotter. Why?"

Emma McChesney had the telephone operator before he could finish.

"Get me Trotter, the tailor, T-r-o-double-t-e-r. Say I want to speak to the tailor who fits Mr. Ed Meyers, of the Sans-Silk Skirt Company."

T. A. Buck leaned forward, mouth open, eyes wide. "Well, what in the name of——"

"I'll let you know in a minute. Maybe I'm wrong. It's just one of my hunches. But for

[5]

ten years I sold Featherlooms through the same territory that Ed Meyers was covering for the Sans-Silk Skirt people. It didn't take me ten years to learn that Fat Ed hadn't the decency to be ashamed of any deal he turned, no matter how raw. And let me tell you, T. A.: If he dodged when he saw you it wasn't because he was ashamed of having played us low-down. He was contemplating playing ·lower-down. Of course, I may be——''

She picked up the receiver in answer to the bell. Then, sweetly, her calm eyes smiling into Buck's puzzled ones:

"Hello! Is this Mr. Meyers' tailor? I'm to ask if you are sure that the grade he selected is the proper weight for the tropics. What? Oh, you say you assured him it was the weight of flannel you always advise for South America. And you said they'd be ready when? Next week? Thank you."

She hung up the receiver. The pupils of her eyes were dilated. Her cheeks were very pink as always under excitement. She stood up, her breath coming rather quickly.

"Hurray for the hunch! It holds. Fat Ed Meyers is going down to South America for the

Sans-Silk Company. It's what I've been planning to do for the last six months. You remember I spoke of it. You pooh-poohed the idea. It means hundreds of thousands of dollars to the Sans-Silk people if they get it. But they won't get it."

T. A. Buck stood up suddenly.

"Look here, Emma! If you're——"

"I certainly am. Nothing can stop me. The skirt business has been—well, you know what it's been for the last two years. The South American boats sail twice a month. Fat Ed Meyers' clothes are promised for next week. That means he isn't sailing until week after next. But the next boat sails in three days." She picked up a piece of paper from her desk and tossed it into Buck's hand. "That's the letter I was reading when you came in. No; don't read it. Let me tell you instead."

Buck threw cane, hat, gloves, and letter on the broad desk, thrust his hands into his pockets, and prepared for argument. But he got only as far as: "But I won't allow it! You couldn't get away in three days, at any rate. And at the end of two weeks you'll have come to your senses, and besides——"

[7]

"T. A., I don't mean to be rude. But here are your hat and stick and gloves. It's going to take me just forty-eight hours to mobilize."

"But, Emma, even if you do get in ahead of Meyers, it's an insane idea. A woman can't go down there alone. It isn't safe. It's bad enough for a man to tackle it. Besides, we're holding our own."

"That's just it. When a doctor issues a bulletin to the effect that the patient is holding his own, you may have noticed that the relatives always begin to gather."

"It's a bubble, this South American idea. Oshkosh and Southport and Altoona money has always been good enough for us. If we can keep that trade, we ought to be thankful."

Emma McChesney pushed her hair back from her forehead with one gesture and patted it into place with another. Those two gestures, to one who knew her, meant loss of composure for one instant, followed by the quick regaining of it the next.

"Let's not argue about it now. Suppose we wait until to-morrow—when it's too late. I am thankful for the trade we've got. But I don't want to be narrow about it. My thanking capacity is such that I can stretch it out to cover some things we haven't got yet. I've been reading up on South America."

"Reading!" put in Buck hotly. "What actual first-hand information can you get about a country from books?"

"Well, then, I haven't only been reading. I've been talking to everyone I could lay my hands on who has been down there and who knows. Those South American women love dress—especially the Argentines. And do you know what they've been wearing? Petticoats made in England! You know what that means. An English woman chooses a petticoat like she does a husband—for life. It isn't only a garment. It's a shelter. It's built like a tent. If once I can introduce the T. A. Buck Featherloom petticoat and knickerbocker into sunny South America, they'll use those English and German petticoats for linoleum floor-coverings. Heaven knows they'll fit the floor better than the human form!"

But Buck was unsmiling. The muscles of his jaw were tense.

"I won't let you go. Understand that! I won't allow it!"

"Tut, tut, T. A.! What is this? Cave-man stuff?"

"Emma, I tell you it's dangerous. It isn't worth the risk, no matter what it brings us."

Emma McChesney struck an attitude, hand on heart. " 'Heaven will protect the working girrul,' " she sang.

Buck grabbed his hat.

"I'm going to wire Jock."

"All right! That'll save me fifty cents. Do you know what he'll wire back? 'Go to it. Get the tango on its native tairn'—or words to that effect."

"Emma, use a little logic and common sense!"

There was a note in Buck's voice that brought a quick response from Mrs. McChesney. She dropped her little air of gayety. The pain in his voice, and the hurt in his eyes, and the pleading in his whole attitude banished the smile from her face. It had not been much of a smile, anyway. T. A. knew her genuine smiles well enough to recognize a counterfeit at sight. And Emma McChesney knew that he knew. She came over and laid a hand lightly on his arm.

"T. A., I don't know anything about logic.

It is a hot-house plant. But common sense is a field flower, and I've gathered whole bunches of it in my years of business experience. I'm not going down to South America for a lark. I'm going because the time is ripe to go. I'm going because the future of our business needs it. I'm going because it's a job to be handled by the most experienced salesman on our staff. And I'm just that. I say it because it's true. Your father, T. A., used to see things straighter and farther than any business man I ever knew. Since his death made me a partner in this firm, I find myself, when I'm troubled or puzzled, trying to see a situation as he'd see it if he were alive. It's like having an expert stand back of you in a game of cards, showing you the next move. That's the way I'm playing this hand. And I think we're going to take most of the tricks away from Fat Ed Meyers."

T. A. Buck's eyes traveled from Emma Mc-Chesney's earnest, glowing face to the hand that rested on his arm. He reached over and gently covered that hand with his own.

"I suppose you must be right, little woman. You always are. Dad was the founder of this business. It was the pride of his life. That word 'founder' has two meanings. I never want to be responsible for its second meaning in connection with this concern."

"You never will be, T. A."

"Not with you at the helm." He smiled rather sadly. "I'm a good, ordinary, common seaman. But you've got imagination, and foresight, and nerve, and daring, and that's the stuff that admirals are made of."

"Bless you, T. A.! I knew you'd see the thing as I do after the first shock was over. It has always been nip and tuck between the Sans-Silk Company and us. You gave me the hint that showed me their plans. Now help me follow it up."

Buck picked up his hat, squared his shoulders and fumbled with his gloves like a bashful schoolboy.

"You—you couldn't kill two birds with one stone on this trip, could you, Mrs. Mack?"

Mrs. McChesney, back at her desk again, threw him an inquiring glance over her shoulder.

"You might make it a combination honeymoon and Featherloom expedition."

"T. A. Buck!" exclaimed Emma McChesney.

Then, as Buck dodged for the door: "Just for that, I'm going to break this to you. You know that I intended to handle the Middle Western territory for one trip, or until we could get a man to take Fat Ed Meyers' place."

"Well?" said Buck apprehensively.

"I leave in three days. Goodness knows how long I'll be gone! A business deal down there is a ceremony. And—you won't need any white-flannel clothes in Rock Island, Illinois."

Buck, aghast, faced her from the doorway. "You mean, I——"

"Just that," smiled Emma McChesney pleasantly. And pressed the button that summoned the stenographer.

In the next forty-eight hours, Mrs. McChesney performed a series of mental and physical calisthenics that would have landed an ordinary woman in a sanatorium. She cleaned up with the thoroughness and dispatch of a housewife who, before going to the seashore, forgets not instructions to the iceman, the milkman, the janitor, and the maid. She surveyed her territory, behind and before, as a general studies troops and countryside before going into battle; she foresaw factory emergencies, dictated office

[13]

policies, made sure of staff organization like the business woman she was. Out in the stock-room, under her supervision, there was scientifically packed into sample-trunks and cases a line of Featherloom skirts and knickers calculated to dazzle Brazil and entrance Argentina. And into her own personal trunk there went a wardrobe, each article of which was a garment with a purpose. Emma McChesney knew the value of a smartly tailored suit in a business argument.

T. A. Buck canceled his order at the tailor's, made up his own line for the Middle West, and prepared to storm that prosperous and important territory for the first time in his business career.

The South American boat sailed Saturday afternoon. Saturday morning found the two partners deep in one of those condensed, last-minute discussions. Mrs. McChesney opened a desk drawer, took out a leather-covered pocket notebook, and handed it to Buck. A tiny smile quivered about her lips. Buck took it, mystified.

"Your last diary?"

"Something much more important. I call it

'The Salesman's Who's Who.' Read it as you ought your Bible."

"But what?" Buck turned the pages wonderingly. He glanced at a paragraph, frowned, read it aloud, slowly.

"Des Moines, Iowa, Klein & Company. Miss Ella Sweeney, skirt buyer. Old girl. Skittish. Wants to be entertained. Take her to dinner and the theater."

He looked up, dazed. "Good Lord, what is this? A joke?"

"Wait until you see Ella; you won't think it's a joke. She'll buy only your smoothest numbers, ask sixty days' dating, and expect you to entertain her as you would your rich aunt."

Buck returned to the little book dazedly. He flipped another leaf—another. Then he read in a stunned sort of voice:

"Sam Bloom, Paris Emporium, Duluth. See Sadie."

He closed the book. "Say, see here, Emma, do you mean to——"

"Sam is the manager," interrupted Mrs. McChesney pleasantly, "and he thinks he does the buying, but the brains of that business is a little girl named Sadie Harris. She's a wonder. Five years from now, if she doesn't marry Sam, she'll be one of those ten-thousand-a-year foreign buyers. Play your samples up to Sammy, but quote your prices down to Sadie. Read the next one, T. A."

Buck read on, his tone lifeless:

"Miss Sharp. Berg Brothers, Omaha. Strictly business. Known among the trade as the human cactus. Canceled a ten-thousand-dollar order once because the grateful salesman called her 'girlie.' Stick to skirts."

Buck slapped the book smartly against the palm of his hand.

"Do you mean to tell me that you made this book out for me? Do you mean to say that I have to cram on this like a kid studying for exams? That I'll have to cater to the personality of the person I'm selling to? Why—it's —it's——"

Emma McChesney nodded calmly.

"I don't know how this trip of yours is going to affect the firm's business, T. A. But it's going to be a liberal education for you. You'll

find that you'll need that little book a good
many times before you're through. And while
you're following its advice, do this: forget that
your name is Buck, except for business pur-
poses; forget that your family has always lived
in a brownstone mausoleum in Seventy-second
street; forget that you like your chops done just
so, and your wine at such-and-such a temperature; get close to your trade. They're an aw-
fully human lot, those Middle Western buyers.
Don't chuck them under the chin, but smile on
'em. And you've got a lovely smile, T. A."

Buck looked up from the little leather book.
And, as he gazed at Emma McChesney, the
smile appeared and justified its praise.

"I'll have this to comfort me, anyway,
Emma. I'll know that while I'm smirking on
the sprightly Miss Sweeney, your face will be
undergoing various agonizing twists in the effort to make American prices understood by an
Argentine who can't speak anything but Spanish."

"Maybe I am short on Spanish, but I'm long
on Featherlooms. I may not know a *señora*
from a *chili con carne,* but I know Featherlooms
from the waistband to the hem." She leaned

forward, dimpling like fourteen instead of forty. "And you've noticed—haven't you, T. A.?—that I've got an expressive countenance."

Buck leaned forward, too. His smile was almost gone.

"I've noticed a lot of things, Emma McChesney. And if you persist in deviling me for one more minute, I'm going to mention a few."

Emma McChesney surveyed her cleared desk, locked the top drawer with a snap, and stood up.

"If you do I'll miss my boat. Just time to make Brooklyn. Suppose you write 'em."

That Ed Meyers might know nothing of her sudden plans, she had kept the trip secret. Besides Buck and the office staff, her son Jock was the only one who knew. But she found her cabin stocked like a prima donna's on a farewell tour. There were boxes of flowers, a package of books, baskets of fruit, piles of magazines, even a neat little sheaf of telegrams, one from the faithful bookkeeper, one from the workroom foreman, two from salesmen long in the firm's employ, two from Jock in Chicago. She read them, her face glowing. He and Buck had vied with each other in supplying her with lux-

uries that would make pleasanter the twenty-
three days of her voyage.

She looked about the snug cabin, her eyes
suddenly misty. Buck poked his head in at
the door.

"Come on up on deck, Emma; I've only a
few minutes left."

She snatched a pink rose from the box, and
together they went on deck.

"Just ten minutes," said Buck. He was looking down at her. "Remember, Emma, nothing
that concerns the firm's business, however big,
is half as important as the things that concern
you personally, however small. I realize what
this trip will mean to us, if it pans, and if you
can beat Meyers to it. But if anything should
happen to you, why——"

"Nothing's going to happen, T. A., except
that I'll probably come home with my complexion ruined. I'll feel a great deal more
at home talking pidgin-English to Señor Al-
varez in Buenos Aires than you will talking
Featherlooms to Miss Skirt-Buyer in Cedar
Rapids, Iowa. But remember this, T. A.:
When you get to know—really to know—the
Sadie Harrises and the Sammy Blochs and the

Ella Sweeneys of this world, you've learned just about all there is to know about human beings. Quick—the gangplank! Goodby, T. A."

The dock reached, he gazed up at her as she leaned far over the railing. He made a megaphone of his hands.

"I feel like an old maid who's staying home with her knitting," he called.

The boat began to move. Emma McChesney passed a quick hand over her eyes.

"Don't drop any stitches, T. A." With unerring aim she flung the big pink rose straight at him.

She went about arranging her affairs on the boat like the business woman that she was. First she made her cabin shipshape. She placed nearest at hand the books on South America, and the Spanish-American pocket interpreter. She located her deck chair, and her seat in the dining-room. Then, quietly, unobtrusively, and guided by those years spent in meeting men and women face to face in business, she took thorough, conscientious mental stock of those others who were to be her fellow travelers for twenty-three days.

For the most part, the first-class passengers

were men. There were American business men
—salesmen, some of them, promoters others,
or representatives of big syndicates—shrewd,
alert, well dressed, smooth shaven. Emma Mc-
Chesney knew that she would gain valuable
information from many of them before the trip
was over. She sighed a little regretfully as she
thought of those smoking-room talks—those
intimate, tobacco-mellowed business talks from
which she would be barred by her sex.

There were two engineers, one British, one
American, both very intelligent-looking, both
inclined to taciturnity, as is often the case in
men of their profession. They walked a good
deal, and smoked nut-brown, evil-smelling pipes,
and stared unblinkingly across the water.

There were Argentines—whole families of
them—Brazilians, too. The fat, bejeweled
Brazilian men eyed Emma McChesney with
open approval, even talked to her, leering ob-
jectionably. Emma McChesney refused to be
annoyed. Her ten years on the road served
her in good stead now.

But most absorbing of all to Emma McChesney, watching quietly over her book or magazine, was a tall, erect, white-bearded Argen-

tine who, with his family, occupied chairs near hers. His name had struck her with the sound of familiarity when she read it on the passenger list. She had asked the deck-steward to point out the name's owner. "Pagés," she repeated to herself, worriedly, "Pagés? P——" Suddenly she knew. Pagés y Hernandez, the owner of the great Buenos Aires shop—a shop finer than those of Paris. And this was Pagés! All the Featherloom instinct in Emma McChesney came to the surface and stayed there, seething.

That was the morning of the second day out. By afternoon, she had bribed and maneuvered so that her deck chair was next that of the Pagés-family flock of chairs. Señor Pagés reminded her of one of those dashing, white-haired, distinguished-looking men whose likeness graces the cover of a box of your favorite cigars. General Something-or-other-ending-in-z he should have been, with a revolutionary background. He dressed somberly in black, like most of the other Argentine men on board. There was Señora Pagés, very fat, very indolent, very blank, much given to pink satin and diamonds at dinner. Señorita Pagés, over-powdered, overfrizzed, marvelously gowned, with overplumpness just a few years away, sat quietly by Señora Pagés' side, but her darting, flashing, restless eyes were never still. The son (Emma heard them call him Pepe) was barely eighteen, she thought, but quite a man of the world, with his cigarettes, his drinks, his bold eyes. She looked at his sallow, pimpled skin, his lean, brown hands, his lack-luster eyes, and she thought of Jock and was happy.

Mrs. McChesney knew that she might visit the magnificent Buenos Aires shop of Pagés y Hernandez day after day for months without ever obtaining a glimpse of either Pagés or Hernandez. And here was Señor Pagés, so near that she could reach out and touch him from her deck chair. Here was opportunity! A caller who had never been obliged to knock twice at Emma McChesney's door.

Her methods were so simple that she herself smiled at them. She donned her choicest suit of white serge that she had been saving for shore wear. Its skirt had been cut by the very newest trick. Its coat was the kind to make you go home and get out your own white serge and gaze at it with loathing. Señorita Pagés' eyes leaped to that suit as iron leaps to the magnet. Emma McChesney, passing her deck chair, detached the eyes with a neat smile. Why hadn't she spent six months neglecting Skirts for Spanish? she asked herself, groaning. As she approached her own deck chair again she risked a bright, "Good morning." Her heart bounded, stood still, bounded again, as from the lips of the assembled Pagés there issued a combined, courteous, perfectly good American, "Good morning!"

"You speak English!" Emma McChesney's tone expressed flattery and surprise.

Pagés *père* made answer.

"Ah, yes, it is necessary. There are many English in Argentina."

A sigh—a fluttering, tremulous sigh of perfect peace and happiness—welled up from Emma McChesney's heart and escaped through her smiling lips.

By noon, Señorita Pagés had tried on the fascinating coat and secured the address of its builder. By afternoon, Emma McChesney was showing the newest embroidery stitch to the slow but docile Señora Pagés. Next morning she was playing shuffleboard with the elegant, indolent Pepe, and talking North American football and baseball to him. She had not been Jock McChesney's mother all those years for nothing. She could discuss sports with the best of them. Young Pagés was avidly interested. Outdoor sports had become the recent fashion among the rich young Argentines.

The problem of papa Pagés was not so easy. Emma McChesney approached her subject warily, skirting the bypaths of politics, war, climate, customs—to business. Business!

"But a lady as charming as you can understand nothing of business," said Señor Pagés. "Business is for your militant sisters."

"But we American women do understand business. Many—many charming American women are in business."

Señor Pagés turned his fine eyes upon her. She had talked most interestingly, this pretty American woman.

"Perhaps—but pardon me if I think not. A woman cannot be really charming and also capable in business."

Emma McChesney dimpled becomingly.

"But I know a woman who is as—well, as charming as you say I am. Still, she is known as a capable, successful business woman. She'll be in Buenos Aires when I am."

Señor Pagés shook an unbelieving head. Emma McChesney leaned forward.

"Will you let me bring her in to meet you, just to prove my point?"

"She must be as charming as you are." His Argentine betting proclivities rose. "Here; we shall make a wager!" He took a card from his pocket, scribbled on it, handed it to Emma McChesney. "You will please present that to my secretary, who will conduct you immediately to my office. We will pretend it is a friendly call. Your friend need not know. If I lose——"

"If you lose, you must promise to let her show you her sample line."

"But, dear madam, I do no buying."

"Then you must introduce her favorably to the department buyer of her sort of goods."

"But if I win?" persisted Señor Pagés.

"If she isn't as charming as—as you say I am, you may make your own terms."

Señor Pagés' fine eyes opened wide.

It was on the fourteenth day of their trip that they came into quaint Bahia. The stay there was short. Brazilian business methods are long. Emma McChesney took no chances with sample-trunks or cases. She packed her three leading samples into her own personal suitcase, eluded the other tourists, secured an interpreter, and prepared to brave Bahia. She returned just in time to catch the boat, flushed, tired, and orderless. Bahia would have none of her.

In three days they would reach Rio de Janeiro, the magnificent. They would have three days there. She told herself that Bahia didn't count, anyway—sleepy little half-breed town! But the arrow rankled. It had been the first to penetrate the armor of her business success. But she had learned things from that experience at Bahia. She had learned that the South American dislikes the North American because his Northern cousin patronizes him. She learned that the North American business firm is thought by the Southern business man to be tricky and dishonest, and that, because the Northerner has not learned how to pack a case of goods scientifically, as have the English, Germans, and French, the South American rages to pay cubic-feet rates on boxes that are three-quarters empty.

So it was with a heavy heart but a knowing head that she faced Rio de Janeiro. They had entered in the evening, the sunset splashing the bay and the hills in the foreground and the Sugar-loaf Mountain with an unbelievable riot of crimson and gold and orange and blue. Suddenly the sun jerked down, as though pulled by a string, and the magic purple night came up as though pulled by another.

"Well, anyway, I've seen that," breathed Emma McChesney thankfully.

Next morning, she packed her three samples, as before, her heart heavy, her mind on Fat Ed Meyers coming up two weeks behind her. Three days in Rio! And already she had bumped her impatient, quick-thinking, quick-acting North American business head up against the stone wall of South American leisureliness and prejudice. She meant no irreverence, no impiety as she prayed, meanwhile packing Nos. 79, 65, and 48 into her personal bag:

"O Lord, let Fat Ed Meyers have Bahia; but please, please help me to land Rio and Buenos Aires!"

Then, in smart tailored suit and hat, interpreter in tow, a prayer in her heart, and excitement blazing in cheeks and eyes, she made her way to the dock, through the customs, into a cab that was to take her to her arena, the broad Avenida.

Exactly two hours later, there dashed into the customs-house a well-dressed woman whose hat was very much over one ear. She was running as only a woman runs when she's made up her mind to get there. She came hotfoot, helter-skelter, regardless of modishly crippling skirt, past officers, past customs officials, into the section where stood the one small sample-trunk that she had ordered down in case of emergency. The trunk had not gone through the customs. It had not even been opened. But Emma McChesney heeded not trifles like that. Rio de Janeiro had fallen for Featherlooms. Those three samples, Nos. 79, 65, and 48, that boasted style, cut, and workmanship never before seen in Rio, had turned the trick. They were as a taste of blood to a hungry lion. Rio wanted more!

Emma McChesney was kneeling before her trunk, had whipped out her key, unlocked it, and was swiftly selecting the numbers wanted from the trays, her breath coming quickly, her deft fingers choosing unerringly, when an indignant voice said, in Portuguese, "It is forbidden!"

Emma McChesney did not glance around. Her head was buried in the depths of the trunk. But her quick ears had caught the word, *"Prohiba!"*

"Speak English," she said, and went on unpacking.

"Inglés!" shouted the official. "No!" Then, with a superhuman effort, as Emma McChesney stood up, her arms laden with Featherloom samples of rainbow hues, *"Pare! Ar-r-r-rest!"*

Mrs. McChesney slammed down the trunk top, locked it, clutched her samples firmly, and faced the enraged official.

"Go 'way! I haven't time to be arrested this morning. This is my busy day. Call around this evening."

Whereupon she fled to her waiting cab, leaving behind her a Brazilian official stunned and raging by turns.

When she returned, happy, triumphant, order-laden, he was standing there, stunned no longer but raging still. Emma McChesney had forgotten all about him. The gold-braided official advanced, mustachios bristling. A volley of Portuguese burst from his long-pent lips. Emma McChesney glanced behind her. Her interpreter threw up helpless hands, replying with a still more terrifying burst of vowels. Bewildered, a little frightened, Mrs. McChesney stood helplessly by. The official laid a none too gentle hand on her shoulder. A little group of lesser officials stood, comic-opera fashion, in the background. And then Emma McChesney's New York training came to her aid. She ignored the voluble interpreter. She remained coolly unruffled by the fusillade of Portuguese. Quietly she opened her hand bag and plunged her fingers deep, deep therein. Her blue eyes gazed confidingly up into the Brazilian's snapping black ones, and as she withdrew her hand from the depths of her purse, there passed from her white fingers to his brown ones that which is the Esperanto of the nations, the universal language understood from Broadway to Brazil. The hand on her shoulder relaxed and fell away.

On deck once more, she encountered the suave Señor Pagés. He stood at the rail surveying Rio's shores with that lip-curling contempt of the Argentine for everything Brazilian. He regarded Emma McChesney's radiant face.

"You are pleased with this—this Indian Rio?"

Mrs. McChesney paused to gaze with him at the receding shores.

"Like it! I'm afraid I haven't seen it. From here it looks like Coney. But it buys like Seattle. Like it! Well, I should say I do!"

"Ah, *señora*," exclaimed Pagés, distressed, "wait! In six days you will behold Buenos Aires. Your New York, Londres, Paris—bah! You shall drive with my wife and daughter through Palermo. You shall see jewels, motors, *toilettes* as never before. And you will visit my establishment?" He raised an emphatic forefinger. "But surely!"

Emma McChesney regarded him solemnly.

"I promise to do that. You may rely on me."

Six days later they swept up the muddy and majestic Plata, whose color should have won it the name of River of Gold instead of River of

Silver. From the boat's upper deck, Emma McChesney beheld a sky line which was so like the sky line of her own New York that it gave her a shock. She was due for still another shock when, an hour later, she found herself in a maelstrom of motors, cabs, street cars, newsboys, skyscrapers, pedestrians, policemen, subway stations. Where was the South American languor? Where the Argentine inertia? The rush and roar of it, the bustle and the bang of it made the twenty-three-day voyage seem a myth.

"I'm going to shut my eyes," she told herself, "and then open them quickly. If that little brown traffic-policeman turns out to be a big, red-faced traffic-policeman, then I'm right, and this *is* Broadway and Forty-second."

Shock number three came upon her entrance at the Grande Hotel. It had been Emma McChesney's boast that her ten years on the road had familiarized her with every type, grade, style, shape, cut, and mold of hotel clerk. She knew him from the Knickerbocker to the Eagle House at Waterloo, Iowa. At the moment she entered the Grande Hotel, she knew she had overlooked one. Accustomed though she was to the sartorial splendors of the man behind the desk, she might easily have mistaken this one for the president of the republic. In his glittering uniform, he looked a pass between the supreme chancellor of the K.P.'s in full regalia and a prince of India during the Durbar. He was regal. He was overwhelming. He would have made the most splendid specimen of North American hotel clerk look like a scullery boy. Mrs. McChesney spent two whole days in Buenos Aires before she discovered that she could paralyze this personage with a peso. A peso is forty-three cents.

Her experience at Bahia and at Rio de Janeiro had taught her things. So for two days, haunted, as she was, by visions of Fat Ed Meyers coming up close behind her, she possessed her soul in patience and waited. On the great firm of Pagés y Hernandez rested the success of this expedition. When she thought of her little trick on Señor Pagés, her blithe spirits sank. Suppose, after all, that this powerful South American should resent her little Yankee joke!

Her trunks went through the customs. She secured an interpreter. She arranged her sam-

ples with loving care. Style, cut, workmanship
—she ran over their strong points in her mind.
She looked at them as a mother's eyes rest
fondly on the shining faces, the well-brushed
hair, the clean pinafores of her brood. And
her heart swelled with pride. They lay on
their tables, the artful knickerbockers, the
gleaming petticoats, the pink and blue pajamas,
the bifurcated skirts. Emma McChesney ran
one hand lightly over the navy blue satin folds
of a sample.

"Pagés or no Pagés, you're a credit to your
mother," she said, whimsically.

Up in her room once more, she selected her
smartest tailor costume, her most modish hat,
the freshest of gloves and blouses. She chose
the hours between four and six, when wheel
traffic was suspended in the Calle Florida and
throughout the shopping-district, the narrow
streets of which are congested to the point of
suffocation at other times

As she swung down the street they turned to
gaze after her—these Argentines. The fat
señoras turned, and the smartly costumed, sallow *señoritas,* and the men—all of them. They
spoke to her, these last, but she had expected

that, and marched on with her free, swinging stride, her chin high, her color very bright. Into the great shop of Pagés y Hernandez at last, up to the private offices, her breath coming a little quickly, into the presence of the shiny secretary—shiny teeth, shiny hair, shiny skin, shiny nails. He gazed upon Emma McChesney, the shine gleaming brighter. He took in his slim, brown fingers the card on which Señor Pagés had scribbled that day on board ship. The shine became dazzling. He bowed low and backed his way into the office of Señor Pagés.

A successful man is most impressive when in those surroundings which have been built up by his success. On shipboard, Señor Pagés had been a genial, charming, distinguished fellow passenger. In his luxurious business office he still was genial, charming, but his environment seemed to lend him a certain austerity.

"Señora McChesney!"

("How awful that sounds!" Emma McChesney told herself.)

"We spoke of you but last night. And now you come to win the wager, yes?" He smiled, but shook his head.

"Yes," replied Emma McChesney. And tried to smile, too.

Señor Pagés waved a hand toward the outer office.

"She is with you, this business friend who is also so charming?"

"Oh, yes," said Emma McChesney, "she's —she's with me." Then, as he made a motion toward the push-button, which would summon the secretary: "No, don't do that! Wait a minute!" From her bag she drew her business card, presented it. "Read that first."

Señor Pagés read it. He looked up. Then he read it again. He gazed again at Emma McChesney. Emma McChesney looked straight at him and tried in vain to remember ever having heard of the South American's sense of humor. A moment passed. Her heart sank. Then Señor Pagés threw back his fine head and laughed—laughed as the Latin laughs, emphasizing his mirth with many ejaculations and gestures.

"Ah, you Northerners! You are too quick for us. Come; I myself must see this garment which you honor by selling." His glance rested approvingly on Emma McChesney's trim, smart figure. "That which you sell, it must be quite right."

"I not only sell it," said Emma McChesney; "I wear it."

"That—how is it you Northerners say?—ah, yes—that settles it!"

Six weeks later, in his hotel room in Columbus, Ohio, T. A. Buck sat reading a letter forwarded from New York and postmarked Argentina. As he read he chuckled, grew serious, chuckled again and allowed his cigar to grow cold.

For the seventh time:

DEAR T. A.:

They've fallen for Featherlooms the way an Eskimo takes to gum-drops. My letter of credit is all shot to pieces, but it was worth it. They make you pay a separate license fee in each province, and South America is just one darn province after another. If they'd lump a peddler's license for $5,000 and tell you to go ahead, it would be cheaper.

I landed Pagés y Hernandez by a trick. The best of it is the man I played it on saw the point and laughed with me. We North Americans brag too much about our sense of humor.

I thought ten years on the road had hardened me

to the most fiendish efforts of a hotel *chef*. But the food at the Grande here makes a quarter-inch round steak with German fried look like Sherry's latest triumph. You know I'm not fussy. I'm the kind of woman who, given her choice of ice cream or cheese for dessert, will take cheese. Here, given my choice, I play safe and take neither. I've reached the point where I make a meal of radishes. They kill their beef in the morning and serve it for lunch. It looks and tastes like an Ethiop's ear. But I don't care, because I'm getting gorgeously thin.

If the radishes hold out I'll invade Central America and Panama. I've one eye on Valparaiso already. I know it sounds wild, but it means a future and a fortune for Featherlooms. I find I don't even have to talk skirts. They're self-sellers. But I have to talk honesty and packing.

How did you hit it off with Ella Sweeney? Haven't seen a sign of Fat Ed Meyers. I'm getting nervous. Do you think he may have exploded at the equator?

EMMA.

But kind fortune saw fit to add a last sweet drop to Emma McChesney's already brimming cup. As she reached the docks on the day of her departure, clad in cool, crisp white from hat to shoes, her quick eye spied a red-faced, rotund, familiar figure disembarking from the New York boat, just arrived. The fates, grinning, had planned this moment like a stage-manager. Fat Ed Meyers came heavily down the gangplank. His hat was off. He was mopping the top of his head with a large, damp handkerchief. His gaze swept over the busy landing-docks, darted hither and thither, alighted on Emma McChesney with a shock, and rested there. A distinct little shock went through that lady, too. But she waited at the foot of her boat's gangway until the unbelievably nimble Meyers reached her.

He was a fiery spectacle. His cheeks were distended, his eyes protuberant. He wasted no words. They understood each other, those two.

"Coming or going?"

"Going," replied Emma McChesney.

"Clean up this—this Bonez Areez, too?"

"Absolutely."

"Did, huh?"

Meyers stood a moment panting, his little eyes glaring into her calm ones.

"Well, I beat you in Bahia, anyway," he boasted.

Emma McChesney snapped her fingers blithely.

"Bah, for Bahia!" She took a step or two up the gangplank, and turned. "Good-by, Ed. And good luck. I can recommend the radishes, but pass up the beef. Dangerous."

Fat Ed Meyers, still staring, began to stutter unintelligibly, his lips moving while no words came. Emma McChesney held up a warning hand.

"Don't do that, Ed! Not in this climate! A man of your build, too! I'm surprised. Consider the feelings of your firm!"

Fat Ed Meyers glared up at the white-clad, smiling, gracious figure. His hands unclenched. The words came.

"Oh, if only you were a man for just ten minutes!" he moaned.

II

THANKS TO MISS MORRISSEY

IT was Fat Ed Meyers, of the Sans-Silk Skirt Company, who first said that Mrs. Emma McChesney was the Maude Adams of the business world. It was on the occasion of his being called to the carpet for his failure to make Sans-silks as popular as Emma McChesney's famed Featherlooms. He spoke in self-defense, heatedly.

"It isn't Featherlooms. It's McChesney. Her line is no better than ours. It's her personality, not her petticoats. She's got a following that swears by her. If Maude Adams was to open on Broadway in 'East Lynne,' they'd flock to see her, wouldn't they? Well, Emma McChesney could sell hoop-skirts, I'm telling you. She could sell bustles. She could sell red-woolen mittens on Fifth Avenue!"

The title stuck.

It was late in September when Mrs. McChesney, sunburned, decidedly under weight, but

[42]

gloriously triumphant, returned from a four
months' tour of South America. Against the
earnest protests of her business partner, T. A.
Buck, president of the Buck Featherloom Petticoat Company, she had invaded the southern
continent and left it abloom with Featherlooms
from the Plata to the Canal.

Success was no stranger to Mrs. McChesney.
This last business victory had not turned her
head. But it had come perilously near to tilt-
ing that extraordinarily well-balanced part. A
certain light in her eyes, a certain set of her
chin, an added briskness of bearing, a cocky
slant of the eyebrow revealed the fact that,
though Mrs. McChesney's feet were still on
the ground, she might be said to be standing on
tiptoe.

When she had sailed from Brooklyn pier
that June afternoon, four months before, she
had cast her ordinary load of business respon-
sibilities on the unaccustomed shoulders of T.
A. Buck. That elegant person, although president of the company which his father had
founded, had never been its real head. When
trouble threatened in the workroom, it was to
Mrs. McChesney that the forewoman came.

When an irascible customer in Green Bay, Wisconsin, waxed impatient over the delayed shipment of a Featherloom order, it was to Emma McChesney that his typewritten protest was addressed. When the office machinery needed mental oiling, when a new hand demanded to be put on silk-work instead of mercerized, when a consignment of skirt-material turned out to be more than usually metallic, it was in Mrs. Emma McChesney's little private office that the tangle was unsnarled.

She walked into that little office, now, at nine o'clock of a brilliant September morning. It was a reassuring room, bright, orderly, workmanlike, reflecting the personality of its owner. She stood in the center of it now and looked about her, eyes glowing, lips parted. She raised her hands high above her head, then brought them down to her sides again with an unconsciously dramatic gesture that expressed triumph, peace, content, relief, accomplishment, and a great and deep satisfaction. T. A. Buck, in the doorway, saw the gesture—and understood.

"Not so bad to get back to it, is it?"

"Bad! It's like a drink of cool spring water

after too much champagne. In those miserable South American hotels, how I used to long for the orderliness and quiet of this!"

She took off hat and coat. In a vase on the desk, a cluster of yellow chrysanthemums shook their shaggy heads in welcome. Emma McChesney's quick eye jumped to them, then to Buck, who had come in and was surveying the scene appreciatively.

"You—of course." She indicated the flowers with a nod and a radiant smile.

"Sorry—no. The office staff did that. There's a card of welcome, I believe."

"Oh," said Emma McChesney. The smile was still there, but the radiance was gone.

She seated herself at her desk. Buck took the chair near by. She unlocked a drawer, opened it, rummaged, closed it again, unlocked another. She patted the flat top of her desk with loving fingers.

"I can't help it," she said, with a little shamed laugh; "I'm so glad to be back. I'll probably hug the forewoman and bite a piece out of the first Featherloom I lay hands on. I had to use all my self-control to keep from kissing Jake, the elevator-man, coming up."

Out of the corner of her eye, Emma Mc-
Chesney had been glancing at her handsome
business partner. She had found herself doing
the same thing from the time he had met her
at the dock late in the afternoon of the day before. Those four months had wrought some
subtle change. But what? Where? She
frowned a moment in thought.

Then:

"Is that a new suit, T. A.?"

"This? Lord, no! Last summer's. Put it
on because of this July hangover in September.
Why?"

"Oh, I don't know"—vaguely—"I just—
wondered."

There was nothing vague about T. A. Buck,
however. His old air of leisureliness was gone.
His very attitude as he sat there, erect, brisk,
confident, was in direct contrast to his old,
graceful indolence.

"I'd like to go over the home grounds with
you this morning," he said. "Of course, in our
talk last night, we didn't cover the South American situation thoroughly. But your letters and
the orders told the story. You carried the thing
through to success. It's marvelous! But we

stay-at-homes haven't been marking time during your absence."

The puzzled frown still sat on Emma McChesney's brow. As though thinking aloud, she said,

"Have you grown thinner, or fatter or—something?"

"Not an ounce. Weighed at the club yesterday."

He leaned forward a little, his face suddenly very sober.

"Emma, I want to tell you now that—that mother—she—I lost her just a few weeks after you sailed."

Emma McChesney gave a little cry. She came quickly over to him, and one hand went to his shoulder as she stood looking down at him, her face all sympathy and contrition and sorrow.

"And you didn't write me! You didn't even tell me, last night!"

"I didn't want to distress you. I knew you were having a hard-enough pull down there without additional worries. It happened very suddenly while I was out on the road. I got the wire in Peoria. She died very suddenly and quite painlessly. Her companion, Miss Tate, was with her. She had never been herself since Dad's death."

"And you——"

"I could only do what was to be done. Then I went back on the road. I closed up the house, and now I've leased it. Of course it's big enough for a regiment. But we stayed on because mother was used to it. I sold some of the furniture, but stored the things she had loved. She left some to you."

"To me!"

"You know she used to enjoy your visits so much, partly because of the way in which you always talked of Dad. She left you some jewelry that she was fond of, and that colossal old mahogany buffet that you used to rave over whenever you came up. Heaven knows what you'll do with it! It's a white elephant. If you add another story to it, you could rent it out as an apartment."

"Indeed I shall take it, and cherish it, and polish it up myself every week—the beauty!"

She came back to her chair. They sat a moment in silence. Then Emma McChesney spoke musingly.

"So that was it." Buck looked up. "I sensed something—different. I didn't know. I couldn't explain it."

Buck passed a quick hand over his eyes, shook himself, sat up, erect and brisk again, and plunged, with a directness that was as startling as it was new in him, into the details of Middle Western business.

"Good!" exclaimed Emma McChesney. "It's all very well to know that Featherlooms are safe in South America. But the important thing is to know how they're going in the corn country."

Buck stood up.

"Suppose we transfer this talk to my office. All the papers are there, all the correspondence —all the orders, everything. You can get the whole situation in half an hour. What's the use of talking when figures will tell you."

He walked swiftly over to the door and stood there waiting. Emma McChesney rose. The puzzled look was there again.

"No, that wasn't it, after all," she said.

"Eh?" said Buck. "Wasn't what?"

"Nothing," replied Emma McChesney. "I'm wool-gathering this morning. I'm afraid it's going to take me a day or two to get back into harness again."

"If you'd rather wait, if you think you'll be more fit to-morrow or the day after, we'll wait. There's no real hurry. I just thought——"

But Mrs. McChesney led the way across the hall that separated her office from her partner's. Halfway across, she stopped and surveyed the big, bright, busy main office, with its clacking typewriters and rustle and crackle of papers and its air of concentration.

"Why, you've run up a partition there between Miss Casey's desk and the workroom door, haven't you?"

"Yes; it's much better that way."

"Yes, of course. And—why, where are the boys' desks? Spalding's and Hutchinson's, and —they're all gone!" She turned in amazement. "Break it to me! Aren't we using traveling men any more?"

Buck laughed his low, pleasant laugh.

"Oh, yes; but I thought their desks belonged somewhere else than in the main office. They're now installed in the little room between the shop and Healy's office. Close quarters, but

better than having them out here where they
were inclined to neglect their reports in order
to shine in the eyes of that pretty new stenographer. There are one or two other changes.
I hope you'll approve of them."

"I'm sure I shall," replied Emma McChesney, a little stiffly.

In Buck's office, she settled back in her chair
to watch him as he arranged neat sheaves of
papers for her inspection. Her eyes traveled
from his keen, eager face to the piles of paper
and back again.

"Tell me, did you hit it off with the Ella
Sweeneys and the Sadie Harrises of the great
Middle West? Is business as bad as the howl-
ers say it is? You said something last night
about a novelty bifurcated skirt. Was that the
new designer's idea? How have the early buyers taken to it?"

Buck crooked an elbow over his head in self-
defense.

"Stop it! You make me feel like Rheims
cathedral. Don't bombard until negotiations
fail."

He handed her the first sheaf of papers.
But, before she began to read: "I'll say this

much. Miss Sharp, of Berg Brothers, Omaha —the one you warned against as the human cactus—had me up for dinner. Well, I know you don't, but it's true. Her father and I hit it off just like that. He's a character, that old boy. Ever meet him? No? And Miss Sharp told me something about herself that explains her porcupine pose. That poor child was engaged to a chap who was killed in the Spanish-American war, and she——"

"Kate Sharp!" interrupted Emma McChesney. "Why, T. A. Buck, in all her vinegary, narrow life, that girl has never had a beau, much less——"

Buck's eyebrows came up slightly.

"Emma McChesney, you haven't developed —er—claws, have you?"

With a gasp, Emma McChesney plunged into the papers before her. For ten minutes, the silence of the room was unbroken except for the crackling of papers. Then Emma McChesney put down the first sheaf and looked up at her business partner.

"Is that a fair sample?" she demanded.

"Very," answered T. A. Buck, and handed her another set.

[52]

Another ten minutes of silence. Emma Mc-Chesney reached out a hand for still another set of papers. The pink of repressed excitement was tinting her cheeks.

"They're—they're all like this?"

"Practically, yes."

Mrs. McChesney faced him, her eyes wide, her breath coming fast.

"T. A. Buck," she slapped the papers before her smartly with the back of her hand, "this means you've broken our record for Middle Western sales!"

"Yes," said T. A., quietly. "Dad would have enjoyed a morning like this, wouldn't he?"

Emma McChesney stood up.

"Enjoyed it! He *is* enjoying it. Don't tell me that T. A., Senior, just because he is no longer on earth, has failed to get the joy of knowing that his son has realized his fondest dreams. Why, I can feel him here in this room, I can see those bright brown eyes of his twinkling behind his glasses. Not know it! Of course he knows it."

Buck looked down at the desk, smiling curiously.

"D'you know, I felt that way, too."

Suddenly Emma McChesney began to laugh. It was not all mirth—that laugh. Buck waited.

"And to think that I—I kindly and patronizingly handed you a little book full of tips on how to handle Western buyers, 'The Salesman's Who's Who'—I, who used to think I was the witch of the West when it came to selling! You, on your first selling-trip, have made me look like—like a shoe-string peddler."

Buck put out a hand suddenly.

"Don't say that, Emma. I—somehow it takes away all the pleasure."

"It's true. And now that I know, it explains a lot of things that I've been puzzling about in the last twenty-four hours."

"What kind of things?"

"The way you look and act and think. The way you carry your head. The way you sit in a chair. The very words you use, your gestures, your intonations. They're different."

T. A. Buck, busy with his cigar, laughed a little self-consciously.

"Oh, nonsense!" he said. "You're imagining things."

Which remark, while not a particularly

happy one, certainly was not in itself so unfortunate as to explain why Mrs. McChesney should have turned rather suddenly and bolted into her own office across the hall and closed the door behind her.

T. A. Buck, quite cool and unruffled, viewed her sudden departure quizzically. Then he took his cigar from his mouth and stood eying it a moment with more attention, perhaps, than it deserved, in spite of its fine aroma. When he put it back between his lips and sat down at his desk once more he was smiling ever so slightly.

Then began a new order of things in the offices of the T. A. Buck Featherloom Petticoat Company. Feet that once had turned quite as a matter of course toward the door marked "MRS. McCHESNEY," now took the direction of the door opposite—and that door bore the name of Buck. Those four months of Mrs. McChesney's absence had put her partner to the test. That acid test had washed away the accumulated dross of years and revealed the precious metal beneath. T. A. Buck had proved to be his father's son.

If Mrs. McChesney noticed that the head

office had miraculously moved across the hall, if her sharp ears marked that the many feet that once had paused at her door now stopped at the door opposite, if she realized that instead of, "I'd like your opinion on this, Mrs. McChesney," she often heard the new, "I'll ask Mr. Buck," she did not show it by word or sign.

The first of October found buyers still flocking into New York from every State in the country. Shrewd men and women, these—bargain hunters on a grand scale. Armed with the long spoon of business knowledge, they came to skim the cream from factory and workroom products set forth for their inspection.

For years, it had been Emma McChesney's quiet boast that of those whose business brought them to the offices and showrooms of the T. A. Buck Featherloom Petticoat Company, the foremost insisted on dealing only with her. She was proud of her following. She liked their loyalty. Their preference for her was the subtlest compliment that was in their power to pay. Ethel Morrissey, whose friendship dated back to the days when Emma McChesney had sold Featherlooms through the Middle West, used to say laughingly, her plump, comfortable shoulders shaking, "Emma, if you ever give me away by telling how many years I've been buying Featherlooms of you, I'll—I'll call down upon you the spinster's curse."

Early Monday morning, Mrs. McChesney, coming down the hall from the workroom, encountered Miss Ella Sweeney, of Klein & Company, Des Moines, Iowa, stepping out of the elevator. A very skittish Miss Sweeney, rustling, preening, conscious of her dangling black earrings and her Robespierre collar and her beauty-patch. Emma McChesney met this apparition with outstretched, welcoming hand.

"Ella Sweeney! Well, I'd almost given you up. You're late this fall. Come into my office."

She led the way, not noticing that Miss Sweeney came reluctantly, her eyes on the closed door across the way.

"Sit down," said Emma McChesney, and pulled a chair nearer her desk. "No; wait a minute! Let me look at you. Now, Ella, don't try to tell me that *that* dress came from Des Moines, Iowa! Do I! Why, child, it's distinctive!"

Miss Sweeney, still standing, smiled a

pleased but rather preoccupied smile. Her
eyes roved toward the door.

Emma McChesney, radiating good will and
energy, went on:

"Wait till you see our new samples! You'll
buy a million dollars' worth. Just let me lead
you to our new Walk-Easy bifurcated skirt.
We call it the 'one-stepper's delight.'" She
put a hand on Ella Sweeney's arm, preparatory
to guiding her to the showrooms in the rear.
But Miss Sweeney's strange reluctance grew
into resolve. A blush, as real as it was unaccustomed, arose to her bepowdered cheeks.

"Is—I—that is—Mr. Buck is in, I suppose?"

"Mr. Buck? Oh, yes, he's in."

Miss Sweeney's eyes sought the closed door
across the hall.

"Is that—his office?"

Emma McChesney stiffened a little. Her
eyes narrowed thoughtfully. "You have
guessed it," she said crisply. "Mr. Buck's
name is on the door, and you are looking at it."

Miss Sweeney looked down, looked up,
twiddled the chain about her neck.

"You want to see Mr. Buck?" asked Emma
McChesney quietly.

Miss Sweeney simpered down at her glove-tips, fluttered her eyelids.

"Well—yes—I—I—you see, I bought of him this year, and when you buy of a person, why, naturally, you——"

"Naturally; I understand."

She walked across the hall, threw open the door, and met T. A. Buck's glance coolly.

"Mr. Buck, Miss Sweeney, of Des Moines, is here, and I'm sure you want to see her. This way, Miss Sweeney."

Miss Sweeney, sidling, blushing, fluttering, teetered in. Emma McChesney, just before she closed the door, saw a little spasm cross Buck's face. It was gone so quickly, and a radiant smile sat there so reassuringly, that she wondered if she had not been mistaken, after all. He had advanced, hand outstretched, with:

"Miss Sweeney! It—it's wonderful to see you again! You're looking——"

The closed door stifled the rest. Emma McChesney, in her office across the way, stood a moment in the center of the room, her hand covering her eyes. The hardy chrysanthemums still glowed sunnily from their vase. The little room was very quiet except for the ticking of the smart, leather-encased clock on the desk. The closed door shut out factory and office sounds. And Emma McChesney stood with one hand over her eyes. So Napoleon might have stood after Waterloo.

After this first lesson, Mrs. McChesney did not err again. When, two days later, Miss Sharp, of Berg Brothers, Omaha, breezed in, looking strangely juvenile and distinctly anticipatory, Emma greeted her smilingly and waved her toward the door opposite. Miss Sharp, the erstwhile bristling, was strangely smooth and sleek. She glanced ever so softly, sighed ever so flutteringly.

"Working side by side with him, seeing him day after day, how have you been able to resist him?"

Emma McChesney was only human, after all.

"By remembering that this is a business house, not a matrimonial parlor."

The dart found no lodging place in Miss Sharp's sleek armor. She seemed scarcely to have heard.

"My dear," she whispered, "his eyes! And his manner! You must be—whatchamaycallit

—adamant. Is that the way you pronounce it?
You know what I mean."

"Oh, yes," replied Emma McChesney evenly,
"I—know what you mean."

She told herself that she was justified in the
righteous contempt which she felt for this sort
of thing. A heart-breaker! A cheap lady-
killer! Whereupon in walked Sam Bloom, of
the Paris Emporium, Duluth, one of Mrs. Mc-
Chesney's stanchest admirers and a long-tried
business friend.

The usual thing: "Younger than ever, Mrs.
McChesney! You're a wonder—yes, you are!
How's business? Same here. Going to have
lunch with me to-day?" Then: "I'll just run
in and see Buck. Say, where's he been keep-
ing himself all these years? Chip off the old
block, that boy."

So he had the men, too!

It was in this frame of mind that Miss Ethel
Morrissey found her on the morning that she
came into New York on her semi-annual buying-trip. Ethel Morrissey, plump, matronly-
looking, quiet, with her hair fast graying at the
sides, had nothing of the skittish Middle Western buyer about her. She might have passed

for the mother of a brood of six if it were not for her eyes—the shrewd, twinkling, far-sighted, reckoning eyes of the business woman. She and Emma McChesney had been friends from the day that Ethel Morrissey had bought her first cautious bill of Featherlooms. Her love for Emma McChesney had much of the maternal in it. She felt a personal pride in Emma McChesney's work, her success, her clean reputation, her life of self-denial for her son Jock. When Ethel Morrissey was planned by her Maker, she had not been meant to be wasted on the skirt-and-suit department of a small-town store. That broad, gracious breast had been planned as a resting-place for heads in need of comfort. Those plump, firm arms were meant to enfold the weak and distressed. Those capable hands should have smoothed troubled heads and patted plump cheeks, instead of wasting their gifts in folding piles of petticoats and deftly twitching a plait or a tuck into place. She was playing *Rosalind* in buskins when she should have been cast for the *Nurse*.

She entered Emma McChesney's office, now, in her quiet blue suit and her neat hat, and she looked very sane and cheerful and rosy-cheeked and dependable. At least, so Emma McChesney thought, as she kissed her, while the plump arms held her close.

Ethel Morrissey, the hugging process completed, held her off and eyed her.

"Well, Emma McChesney, flourish your Featherlooms for me. I want to buy and get it over, so we can talk."

"Are you sure that you want to buy of me?" asked Emma McChesney, a little wearily.

"What's the joke?"

"I'm not joking. I thought that perhaps you might prefer to see Mr. Buck this trip."

Ethel Morrissey placed one forefinger under Emma McChesney's chin and turned that lady's face toward her and gazed at her long and thoughtfully—the most trying test of courage in the world, that, to one whose eyes fear meeting yours. Emma McChesney, bravest of women, tried to withstand it, and failed. The next instant her head lay on Ethel Morrissey's broad breast, her hands were clutching the plump shoulders, her cheek was being patted soothingly by the kind hands.

"Now, now—what is it, dear? Tell Ethel.

[63]

Yes; I do know, but tell me, anyway. It'll do you good."

And Emma McChesney told her. When she had finished:

"You bathe your eyes, Emma, and put on your hat and we'll eat. Oh, yes, you will. A cup of tea, anyway. Isn't there some little cool fool place where I can be comfortable on a hot day like this—where we can talk comfortably? I've got at least an hour's conversation in me."

With the first sip of her first cup of tea, Ethel Morrissey began to unload that burden of conversation.

"Emma, this is the best thing that could have happened to you. Oh, yes, it is. The queer thing about it is that it didn't happen sooner. It was bound to come. You know, Emma, the Lord lets a woman climb just so high up the mountain of success. And then, when she gets too cocky, when she begins to measure her wits and brain and strength against that of men, and finds herself superior, he just taps her smartly on the head and shins, so that she stumbles, falls, and rolls down a few miles on the road she has traveled so painfully. He does it just as a gentle reminder to her that she's only a woman, after all. Oh, I know all about this feminist talk. But this thing's been proven. Look at what happened to—to Joan of Arc, and Becky Sharp, and Mary Queen of Scots, and—yes, I have been spending my evenings reading. Now, stop laughing at your old Ethel, Emma McChesney!"

"You meant me to laugh, dear old thing. I don't feel much like it, though. I don't see why I should be reminded of my lowly state. Heaven knows I haven't been so terrifically pleased with myself! Of course, that South American trip was—well, gratifying. But I earned it. For ten years I lived with head in a sample-trunk, didn't I? I worked hard enough to win the love of all these Westerners. It wasn't all walking dreamily down Main Street, strewing Featherlooms along my path."

Ethel Morrissey stirred her second cup of tea, sipped, stirred, smiled, then reached over and patted Emma McChesney's hand.

"Emma, I'm a wise old party, and I can see that it isn't all pique with you. It's something else—something deeper. Oh, yes, it is! Now let me tell you what happened when T. A. Buck invaded your old-time territory. I was busy up

in my department the morning he came in.
I had my head in a rack of coats, and a henny
customer waiting. But I sensed something stir-
ring, and I stuck my head out of the coat-rack
in which I was fumbling. The department was
aflutter like a poultry-yard. Every woman in
it, from the little new Swede stock-girl to
Gladys Hemingway, who is only working to
wear out her old clothes, was standing with her
face toward the elevator, and on her face a
look that would make the ordinary door-mat
marked 'Welcome' seem like an insult. I kind
of smoothed my back hair, because I knew that
only one thing could bring that look into a woman's face. And down the aisle came a tall, slim,
distinguished-looking, wonderfully tailored,
chamois-gloved, walking-sticked Fifth Avenue
person with *eyes!* Of course, I knew. But the
other girls didn't. They just sort of fell back
at his approach, smitten. He didn't even raise
an eyebrow to do it. Now, Emma, I'm not
exaggerating. I know what effect he had on
me and my girls, and, for that matter, every
other man or woman in the store. Why, he
was a dream realized to most of 'em. These
shrewd, clever buyer-girls know plenty of men

—business men of the slap-bang, horn-blowing, bluff, good-natured, hello-kid kind—the kind that takes you out to dinner and blows cigar smoke in your face. Along comes this chap, elegant, well dressed and not even conscious of it, polished, suave, smooth, low-voiced, well bred. Why, when he spoke to a girl, it was the subtlest kind of flattery. Can you see little Sadie Harris, of Duluth, drawing a mental comparison between Sam Bloom, the store-manager, and this fascinating devil—Sam, red-faced, loud-voiced, shirt-sleeving it around the sample-room, his hat pushed 'way back on his head, chewing his cigar like mad, and wild-eyed for fear he's buying wrong? Why, child, in our town, nobody carries a cane except the Elks when they have their annual parade, and old man Schwenkel, who's lame. And yet we all accepted that yellow walking-stick of Buck's. It belonged to him. There isn't a skirt-buyer in the Middle West that doesn't dream of him all night and push Featherlooms in the store all day. Emma, I'm old and fat and fifty, but when I had dinner with him at the Manitoba House that evening, I caught myself making eyes at him, knowing that every woman in the dining-room would have given her front teeth to be where I was."

After which extensive period, Ethel Morrissey helped herself to her third cup of tea. Emma McChesney relaxed a little and laughed a tremulous little laugh.

"Oh, well, I suppose I must not hope to combat such formidable rivals as walking-sticks, chamois gloves, and *eyes*. My business arguments are futile compared to those."

Ethel Morrissey delivered herself of a last shot.

"You're wrong, Emma. Those things helped him, but they didn't sell his line. He sold Featherlooms out of salesmanship, and because he sounded convincing and sincere and business-like—and he had the samples. It wasn't all bunk. It was three-quarters business. Those two make an invincible combination."

An hour later, Ethel Morrissey was shrewdly selecting her winter line of Featherlooms from the stock in the showrooms of the T. A. Buck Company. They went about their business transaction, these two, with the cool abruptness of men, speaking little, and then only of prices, discounts, dating, shipping.

Their luncheon conversation of an hour before seemed an impossibility.

"You'll have dinner with me to-night?" Emma asked. "Up at my apartment, all cozy?"

"Not to-night, dearie. I'll be in bed by eight. I'm not the girl I used to be. Time was when a New York buying-trip was a vacation. Now it's a chore."

She took Emma McChesney's hand and patted it.

"If you've got something real nice for dinner, though, and feel like company, why don't you ask—somebody else that's lonesome."

After which, Ethel Morrissey laughed her wickedest and waved a sudden good-by with a last word about seeing her to-morrow.

Emma McChesney, her color high, entered her office. It was five o'clock. She cleared her desk in half an hour, breathed a sigh of weariness, reached for hat and jacket, donned them, and, turning out her lights, closed her door behind her for the day. At that same instant, T. A. Buck slammed his own door and walked briskly down the hall. They met at the elevator.

They descended in silence. The street gained, they paused uncertainly.

"Won't you stay down and have dinner with me to-night, Emma?"

"Thanks so much, T. A. Not to-night."

"I'm—sorry."

"Good night."

"Good night."

She turned away. He stood there, in the busy street, looking irresolutely and not at all eagerly in the direction of his club, perhaps, or his hotel, or whatever shelter he sought after business hours. Something in his attitude—the loneliness of it, the uncertainty, the indecision —smote Emma McChesney with a great pang. She came swiftly back.

"I wish you'd come home to dinner with me. I don't know what Annie'll give us. Probably bread pudding. She does, when she's left to her own devices. But I—I wish you would." She looked up at him almost shyly.

T. A. Buck took Emma McChesney's arm in a rather unnecessarily firm grip and propelled her, surprised and protesting, in the direction of the nearest vacant taxi.

"But, T. A.! This is idiotic! Why take a

cab to go home from the office on a—a week day?"

"In with you! Besides, I never have a chance to take one from the office on Sunday, do I? Does Annie always cook enough for two?"

Apparently Annie did. Annie was something of a witch, in her way. She whisked about, wrought certain changes, did things with asparagus and mayonnaise, lighted the rose-shaded table-candles. No one noticed that dinner was twenty minutes late.

Together they admired the great mahogany buffet that Emma had miraculously found space for in the little dining-room.

"It glows like a great, deep ruby, doesn't it?" she said proudly. "You should see Annie circle around it with the carpet-sweeper. She knows one bump would be followed by instant death."

Looking back on it, afterward, they remembered that the dinner was a very silent one. They did not notice their wordlessness at the time. Once, when the chops came on, Buck said absently,

"Oh, I had those for l——" Then he stopped abruptly.

Emma McChesney smiled.

"Your mother trained you well," she said.

The October night had grown cool. Annie had lighted a wood fire in the living-room.

"That was what attracted me to this apartment in the first place," Mrs. McChesney said, as they left the dining-room. "A fireplace—a practical, real, wood-burning fireplace in a New York apartment! I'd have signed the lease if the plaster had been falling in chunks and the bathtub had been zinc."

"That's because fireplaces mean home—in our minds," said Buck.

He sat looking into the heart of the glow. There fell another of those comfortable silences.

"T. A., I—I want to tell you that I know I've been acting the cat ever since I got home from South America and found that you had taken charge. You see, you had spoiled me. The thing that has happened to me is the thing that always happens to those who assume to be dictators. I just want you to know, now, that I'm glad and proud and happy because you have come into your own. It hurt me just at first. That was the pride of me. I'm quite

over that now. You're not only president of
the T. A. Buck Company in name. You're its
actual head. And that's as it should be. Long
live the King!"

Buck sat silent a moment. Then,

"I had to do it, Emma." She looked up.
"You have a wonderful brain," said Buck then,
and the two utterances seemed connected in his
mind.

They seemed to bring no great satisfaction
to the woman to whom he addressed them,
however. She thanked him dryly, as women do
when their brain is dragged into an intimate
conversation.

"But," said Buck, and suddenly stood up,
looking at her very intently, "it isn't for your
mind that I love you this minute. I love you
for your eyes, Emma, and for your mouth—
you have the tenderest, most womanly-sweet
mouth in the world—and for your hair, and the
way your chin curves. I love you for your
throat-line, and for the way you walk and talk
and sit, for the way you look at me, and for
the way you don't look at me."

He reached down and gathered Emma Mc-
Chesney, the alert, the aggressive, the capable,

into his arms, quite as men gather the clingingest kind of woman. "And now suppose you
tell me just why and how you love me."

And Emma McChesney told him.

When, at last, he was leaving,

"Don't you think," asked Emma McChesney, her hands on his shoulders, "that you
overdid the fascination thing just the least lee-
tle bit there on the road?"

"Well, but you told me to entertain them,
didn't you?"

"Yes," reluctantly; "but I didn't tell you to
consecrate your life to 'em. The ordinary fat,
middle-aged, every-day traveling man will
never be able to sell Featherlooms in the Middle West again. They won't have 'em. They'll
never be satisfied with anything less than John
Drew after this."

"Emma McChesney, you're not marrying me
because a lot of overdressed, giggling, skittish
old girls have taken a fancy to make eyes at me,
are you!"

Emma McChesney stood up very straight
and tall.

"I'm marrying you, T. A., because you are

"He gathered Emma McChesney into his arms, quite as men
gather the clingingest kind of women"—*Page 74*

a great, big, fine, upstanding, tender, wonder-ful——"

"Oh, well, then that's all right," broke in Buck, a little tremulously.

Emma McChesney's face grew serious.

"But promise me one thing, T. A. Promise me that when you come home for dinner at night, you'll never say, 'Good heavens, I had that for lunch!' "

III

A CLOSER CORPORATION

FRONT offices resemble back kitchens in this: they have always an ear at the keyhole, an eye at the crack, a nose in the air. But between the ordinary front office and the front office of the T. A. Buck Featherloom Petticoat Company there was a difference. The employees at Buck's—from Emil, the errand boy, to old Pop Henderson, who had started as errand boy himself twenty-five years before—possessed the quality of loyalty. They were loyal to the memory of old man Buck, because they had loved and respected him. They were loyal to Mrs. Emma McChesney, because she was Mrs. Emma McChesney (which amounts to the same reason). They were loyal to T. A. Buck, because he was his father's son.

For three weeks the front office had been bewildered. From bewilderment it passed to worry. A worried, bewildered front office is

[76]

not an efficient front office. Ever since Mrs.
McChesney had come off the road, at the death
of old T. A. Buck, to assume the secretaryship
of the company which she had served faith-
fully for ten years, she had set an example for
the entire establishment. She was the pace-
maker. Every day of her life she figuratively
pressed the electric button that set the wheels
to whirring. At nine A.M., sharp, she appeared,
erect, brisk, alert, vibrating energy. Usually,
the office staff had not yet swung into its gait.
In a desultory way, it had been getting into its
sateen sleevelets, adjusting its eye-shades, un-
covering its typewriter, opening its ledgers,
bringing out its files. Then, down the hall,
would come the sound of a firm, light, buoyant
step. An electric thrill would pass through the
front office. Then the sunny, sincere, "Good
morning!"

" 'Morning, Mrs. McChesney!" the front office would chorus back.

The day had begun for the T. A. Buck
Featherloom Petticoat Company.

Hortense, the blond stenographer (engaged
to the shipping-clerk), noticed it first. The
psychology of that is interesting. Hortense

knew that by nine-thirty Mrs. McChesney's desk would be clear and that the buzzer would summon her. Hortense didn't mind taking dictation from T. A. Buck, though his method was hesitating and jerky, and he was likely to employ quite casually a baffling and unaccustomed word, over which Hortense's scampering pencil would pause, struggle desperately, then race on. Hortense often was in for a quick, furtive session with her pocket-dictionary after one of T. A.'s periods. But with Mrs. McChesney, dictation was a joy. She knew what she wanted to say and she always said it. The words she used were short, clean-cut, meaningful Anglo-Saxon words. She never used received when she could use got. Hers was the rapid-fire-gun method, each word sharp, well timed, efficient.

Imagine, then, Hortense staring wide-eyed and puzzled at a floundering, hesitating, absent-minded Mrs. McChesney—a Mrs. McChesney strangely starry as to eyes, strangely dreamy as to mood, decidedly deficient as to dictation. Imagine a Hortense with pencil poised in air a full five minutes, waiting until Mrs. McChesney should come to herself with a start, frown, smile vaguely, pass a hand over her eyes, and say, "Let me see—where was I?"

" 'And we find, on referring to your order, that the goods you mention——' " Hortense would prompt patiently.

"Oh, yes, of course," with an effort. Hortense was beginning to grow alarmed.

In T. A. Buck's office, just across the hall, the change was quite as noticeable, but in another way. His leisurely drawl was gone. His deliberate manner was replaced by a brisk, quick-thinking, quick-speaking one. His words were brief and to the point. He seemed to be riding on the crest of an excitement-wave. And, as he dictated, he smiled.

Hortense stood it for a week. Then she unburdened herself to Miss Kelly, the assistant bookkeeper. Miss Kelly evinced no surprise at her disclosures.

"I was just talking about it to Pop yesterday. She acts worried, doesn't she? And yet, not exactly worried, either. Do you suppose it can be that son of hers—what's his name? Jock."

Hortense shook her head.

"No; he's all right. She had a letter from

him yesterday. He's got a grand position in Chicago, and he's going to marry that girl he was so stuck on here. And it isn't that, either, because Mrs. McChesney likes her. I can tell by the way she talks about her. I ought to know. Look how Henry's ma acted toward me when we were first engaged!"

The front office buzzed with it. It crept into the workroom—into the shipping-room. It penetrated the frowsy head of Jake, the elevator-man. As the days went on and the tempo of the front office slackened with that of the two bright little inner offices, only one member of the whole staff remained unmoved, incurious, taciturn. Pop Henderson listened, one scant old eyebrow raised knowingly, a whimsical half-smile screwing up his wrinkled face.

At the end of three weeks, Hortense, with that display of temperament so often encountered in young ladies of her profession, announced in desperation that, if this thing kept on, she was going to forget herself and jeopardize her position by demanding to know outright what the trouble was.

From the direction of Pop Henderson's inky retreat, there came the sound of a dry chuckle.

A CLOSER CORPORATION

Pop Henderson had been chuckling in just that way for three weeks, now. It was getting on the nerves of his colleagues.

"If you ever spring the joke that's kept you giggling for a month," snapped Hortense, "it'll break up the office."

Pop Henderson removed his eye-shade very deliberately, passed his thin, cramped old hand over his scant gray locks to his bald spot, climbed down stiffly from his stool, ambled to the center of the room, and, head cocked like a knowing old brown sparrow, regarded the pert Hortense over his spectacles and under his spectacles and, finally, through his spectacles.

"Young folks now'days," began Pop Henderson dryly, "are so darned cute and knowin' that when an old fellow cuts in ahead of 'em for once, he likes to hug the joke to himself a while before he springs it." There was no acid in his tone. He was beaming very benignantly down upon the little blond stenographer. "You say that Mrs. Mack is absent-minded-like and dreamy, and that young T. A. acts like he'd swallowed an electric battery. Well, when it comes to that, I've seen you many a time, when

[81]

you didn't know any one was lookin', just sitting
there at your typewriter, with your hands kind
of poised halfway, and your lips sort of parted,
and your eyes just gazing away somewhere off
in the distance for fifteen minutes at a stretch.
And out there in the shipping-room Henry's
singing like a whole minstrel troupe all day
long, when he isn't whistlin' so loud you can
hear him over 's far as Eighth Avenue." Then,
as the red surged up through the girl's fair
skin, "Well?" drawled old Pop Henderson, and
the dry chuckle threatened again. "We-e-ell?"

"Why, Pop Henderson!" exploded Miss
Kelly from her cage. "Why—Pop—Henderson!"

In those six words the brisk and agile-minded
Miss Kelly expressed the surprise and the awed
conviction of the office staff.

Pop Henderson trotted over to the water-
cooler, drew a brimming glass, drank it off,
and gave vent to a great exhaust of breath.
He tried not to strut as he crossed back to his
desk, climbed his stool, adjusted his eye-shade,
and, with a last throaty chuckle, plunged into
his books again.

But his words already were working their

wonders. The office, after the first shock, was flooded with a new atmosphere—a subtle, pervasive air of hushed happiness, of tender solicitude. It went about like a mother who has found her child asleep at play, and who steals away atiptoe, finger on lip, lips smiling tenderly.

The delicate antennæ of Emma McChesney's mind sensed the change. Perhaps she read something in the glowing eyes of her sister-in-love, Hortense. Perhaps she caught a new tone in Miss Kelly's voice or the forewoman's. Perhaps a whisper from the outer office reached her desk. The very afternoon of Pop Henderson's electrifying speech, Mrs. McChesney crossed to T. A. Buck's office, shut the door after her, lowered her voice discreetly, and said,

"T. A., they're on."

"What makes you think so?"

"Nothing. That is, nothing definite. No man-reason. Just a woman-reason."

T. A. Buck strolled over to her, smiling.

"I haven't known you all this time without having learned that that's reason enough. And if they really do know, I'm glad."

"But we didn't want them to know. Not yet—until—until just before the——"

T. A. Buck laid his hands lightly on Emma McChesney's shoulders. Emma McChesney promptly reached up and removed them.

"There you are!" exclaimed Buck, and rammed the offending hands into his pockets. "That's why I'm glad they know—if they really do know. I'm no actor. I'm a skirt-and-lingerie manufacturer. For the last six weeks, instead of being allowed to look at you with the expression that a man naturally wears when he's looking at the woman he's going to marry, what have I had to do? Glare, that's what! Scowl! Act like a captain of finance when I've felt like a Romeo! I've had to be dry, terse, businesslike, when I was bursting with adjectives that had nothing to do with business. You've avoided my office as you would a smallpox camp. You've greeted me with a what-can-I-do-for-you air when I've dared to invade yours. You couldn't have been less cordial to a book agent. If it weren't for those two hours you grant me in the evening, I'd—I'd blow up with a loud report, that's what. I'd——"

"Now, now, T. A.!" interrupted Emma Mc-

Chesney soothingly, and patted one gesticulating arm. "It has been a bit of a strain—for both of us. But, you know, we agreed it would be best this way. We've ten days more to go. Let's stick it out as we've begun. It has been best for us, for the office, for the business. The next time you find yourself choked up with a stock of fancy adjectives, write a sonnet to me. Work 'em off that way."

T. A. Buck stood silent a moment, regarding her with a concentration that would have unnerved a woman less poised.

"Emma McChesney, when you talk like that, so coolly, so evenly, so—so darned mentally, I sometimes wonder if you really——"

"Don't say it, T. A. Because you don't mean it. I've had to fight for most of my happiness. I've never before found it ready at hand. I've always had to dig for it with a shovel and a spade and a pickax, and then blast. I had almost twenty years of that— from the time I was eighteen until I was thirty-eight. It taught me to take my happiness seriously and my troubles lightly." She shut her eyes for a moment, and her voice was very low and very deep and very vibrant. "So, when I'm coolest and evenest and most mental, T. A., you may know that I've struck gold."

A great glow illumined Buck's fine eyes. He took two quick steps in her direction. But Emma McChesney, one hand on the door-knob, warned him off with the other.

"Hey—wait a minute!" pleaded Buck.

"Can't. I've a fitting at the tailor's at three-thirty—my new suit. Wait till you see it!"

"The dickens you have! But so have I"—he jerked out his watch—"at three-thirty! It's the suit I'm going to wear when I travel as a blushing bridegroom."

"So's mine. And look here, T. A.! We can't both leave this place for a fitting. It's absurd. If this keeps on, it will break up the business. We'll have to get married one at a time—or, at least, get our trousseaux one at a time. What's your suit?"

"Sort of brown."

"Brown? So's mine! Good heavens, T. A., we'll look like a minstrel troupe!"

Buck sighed resignedly.

"If I telephone my tailor that I can't make it until four-thirty, will you promise to be back by that time?"

A CLOSER CORPORATION

"Yes; but remember, if your bride appears in a skirt that sags in the back or a coat that bunches across the shoulders, the crime will lie at your door."

So it was that the lynx-eyed office staff began to wonder if, after all, Pop Henderson was the wizard that he had claimed to be.

During working hours, Mrs. McChesney held rigidly to business. Her handsome partner tried bravely to follow her example. If he failed occasionally, perhaps Emma McChesney was not so displeased as she pretended to be. A business discussion, deeply interesting to both, was likely to run thus:

Buck, entering her office briskly, papers in hand: "Mrs. McChesney—ahem!—I have here a letter from Singer & French, Columbus, Ohio. They ask for an extension. They've had ninety days."

"That's enough. That firm's slow pay, and always will be until old Singer has the good taste and common sense to retire. It isn't because the stock doesn't move. Singer simply believes in not paying for anything until he has to. If I were you, I'd write him that this is a business house, not a charitable institu-

tion—— No, don't do that. It isn't politic.
But you know what I mean."

"H'm; yes." A silence. "Emma, that's a
fiendishly becoming gown."

"Now, T. A.!"

"But it is! It—it's so kind of loose, and
yet clinging, and those white collar-and-cuff
things——"

"T. A. Buck, I've worn this thing down to
the office every day for a month. It shines in
the back. Besides, you promised not to——"

"Oh, darn it all, Emma, I'm human, you
know! How do you suppose I can stand here
and look at you and not——"

Emma McChesney (pressing the buzzer that
summons Hortense): "You know, Tim, I
don't exactly hate you this morning, either. But
business is business. Stop looking at me like
that!" Then, to Hortense, in the doorway:
"Just take this letter, Miss Stotz—Singer &
French, Columbus, Ohio. Dear Sirs: Yours
of the tenth at hand. Period. Regarding your
request for further extension we wish to say
that, in view of the fact——"

T. A. Buck, half resentful, half amused,
wholly admiring, would disappear. But Hor-

tense, eyes demurely cast down at her note-book, was not deceived.

"Say," she confided to Miss Kelly, "they think they've got me fooled. But I'm wise. Don't I know? When Henry passes through the office here, from the shipping-room, he looks at me just as cool and indifferent. Before we announced it, we had you all guessing, didn't we? But I can see something back of that look that the rest of you can't get. Well, when Mr. Buck looks at her, I can see the same thing in his eyes. Say, when it comes to seeing the love-light through the fog, I'm there with the spy-glass."

If Emma McChesney held herself well in leash during the busy day, she relished her happiness none the less when she could allow herself the full savor of it. When a girl of eighteen she had married a man of the sort that must put whisky into his stomach before the machinery of his day would take up its creaking round. Out of the degradation of that marriage she had emerged triumphantly, sweet and unsullied, and she had succeeded in bringing her son, Jock McChesney, out into the clear sunlight with her.

The evenings spent with T. A. Buck, the man of fine instincts, of breeding, of proven worth, of rare tenderness, filled her with a great peace and happiness. When doubts assailed her, it was not for herself but for him. Sometimes the fear would clutch her as they sat before the fire in the sitting-room of her comfortable little apartment. She would voice those fears for the very joy of having them stilled.

"T. A., this is too much happiness. I'm— I'm afraid. After all, you're a young man, though you are a bit older than I in actual years. But men of your age marry girls of eighteen. You're handsome. And you've brains, family, breeding, money. Any girl in New York would be glad to marry you—those tall, slim, exquisite young girls. Young! And well bred, and poised and fresh and sweet and lovable. You see them every day on Fifth Avenue, exquisitely dressed, entirely desirable. They make me feel —old—old and battered. I've sold goods on the road. I've fought and worked and struggled. And it has left its mark. I did it for the boy, God bless him! And I'm glad I did

it. But it put me out of the class of that girl
you see on——"

"Yes, Emma; you're not at all in the class
with that girl you see every day on Fifth Avenue. Fifth Avenue's full of her—hundreds of
her, thousands of her. Perhaps, five years ago,
before I had worked side by side with you, I
might have been attracted by that girl you see
every day on Fifth Avenue. You don't see a
procession of Emma McChesneys every day on
Fifth Avenue—not by a long shot! Why? Because there's only one of her. She doesn't come
in dozen lots. I know that that girl you see
every day on Fifth Avenue is all that I deserve.
But, by some heaven-sent miracle, I'm to have
this Emma McChesney woman! I don't know
how it came to be true. I don't deserve it.
But it is true, and that's enough for me."

Emma McChesney would look up at him,
eyes wet, mouth smiling.

"T. A., you're balm and myrrh and incense
and meat and drink to me. I wish I had words
to tell you what I'm thinking now. But I
haven't. So I'll just cover it up. We both
know it's there. And I'll tell you that you
make love like a 'movie' hero. Yes, you do!

Better than a 'movie' hero, because, in the films, the heroine always has to turn to face the camera, which makes it necessary for him to make love down the back of her neck."

But T. A. Buck was unsmiling.

"Don't trifle, Emma. And don't think you can fool me that way. I haven't finished. I want to settle this Fifth Avenue creature for all time. What I have to say is this: I think you are more attractive—finer, bigger, more rounded in character and manner, mellower, sweeter, sounder, with all your angles and corners rubbed smooth, saner, better poised than any woman I have ever known. And what I am to-day you have made me, directly and indirectly, by association and by actual orders, by suggestion, and by direct contact. What you did for Jock, purposefully and by force, you did for me, too. Not so directly, perhaps, but with the same result. Emma McChesney, you've made—actually made, molded, shaped, and turned out two men. You're the greatest sculptor that ever lived. You could make a scarecrow in a field get up and achieve. Everywhere one sees women over-wrought, over-stimulated, eager, tense. When there appears one who has herself in leash, balanced, tolerant, poised, sane, composed, she restores your faith in things. You lean on her, spiritually. I know I need you more than you need me, Emma. And I know you won't love me the less for that. There—that's about all for this evening."

"I think," breathed Emma McChesney in a choked little voice, "that that's about—enough."

Two days before the date set for their very quiet wedding, they told the heads of office and workroom. Office and workroom, somewhat moist as to eye and flushed as to cheek and highly congratulatory, proved their knowingness by promptly presenting to their employers a very costly and unbelievably hideous set of mantel ornaments and clock, calculated to strike horror to the heart of any woman who has lovingly planned the furnishing of her drawingroom. Pop Henderson, after some preliminary wrestling with collar, necktie, spectacles, and voice, launched forth on a presentation speech that threatened to close down the works for the day. Emma McChesney heard it, tears in her eyes. T. A. Buck gnawed his mustache.

And when Pop Henderson's cracked old voice broke altogether in the passage that touched on his departed employer, old T. A. Buck, and the great happiness that this occasion would have brought him, Emma's hand met young T. A.'s and rested there. Hortense and Henry, standing very close together all through the speech, had, in this respect, anticipated their employers by several minutes.

They were to be away two weeks only. No one knew just where, except that some small part of the trip was to be spent on a flying visit to young Jock McChesney out in Chicago. He himself was to be married very soon. Emma McChesney had rather startled her very good-looking husband-to-be by whirling about at him with,

"T. A., do you realize that you're very likely to be a step-grandfather some fine day not so far away!"

T. A. had gazed at her for a rather shocked moment, swallowed hard, smiled, and said,

"Even that doesn't scare me, Emma."

Everything had been planned down to the last detail. Mrs. McChesney's little apartment had been subleased, and a very smart one taken

[94]

and furnished almost complete, with Annie installed in the kitchen and a demure parlor-maid engaged.

"When we come back, we'll come home," T. A. Buck had said. "Home!"

There had been much to do, but it had all been done smoothly and expertly, under the direction of these two who had learned how to plan, direct, and carry out.

Then, on the last day, Emma McChesney, visibly perturbed, entered her partner's office, a letter in her hand.

"This is ghastly!" she exclaimed.

Buck pulled out a chair for her.

"Klein cancel his order again?"

"No. And don't ask me to sit down. Be thankful that I don't blow up."

"Is it as bad as that?"

"Bad! Here—read that! No, don't read it; I'll tell you. It'll relieve my feelings. You know how I've been angling and scheming and contriving and plotting for years to get an exclusive order from Gage & Fosdick. Of course we've had a nice little order every few months, but what's that from the biggest mail-order house in the world? And now, out of a blue sky, comes this bolt from O'Malley, who buys our stuff, saying that he's coming on the tenth —that's next week—that he's planned to establish our line with their trade, and that he wants us to be prepared for a record-breaking order. I've fairly prayed for this. And now—what shall we do?"

"Do?"—smoothly—"just write the gentle·man and tell him you're busy getting married this week and next, and that, by a singular co-incidence, your partner is similarly engaged; that our manager will attend to him with all care and courtesy, unless he can postpone his trip until our return. Suggest that he call around a week or two later."

"T. A. Buck, I know it isn't considered good form to rage and glare at one's *fiancé* on the eve of one's wedding-day. If this were a week earlier or a week later, I'd be tempted to— shake you!"

Buck stood up, came over to her, and laid a hand very gently on her arm. With the other hand he took the letter from her fingers.

"Emma, you're tired, and a little excited. You've been under an unusual physical and mental strain for the last few weeks. Give me

that letter. I'll answer it. This kind of thing"
—he held up the letter—"has meant everything
to you. If it had not, where would I be to-day?
But to-night, Emma, it doesn't mean a thing.
Not—one thing."

Slowly Emma McChesney's tense body relaxed. A great sigh that had in it weariness
and relief and acquiescence came from her.
She smiled ever so faintly.

"I've been a ramrod so long it's going to
be hard to learn to be a clinging vine. I've
been my own support for so many years, I don't
use a trellis very gracefully—yet. But I think
I'll get the hang of it very soon."

She turned toward the door, crossed to her
own office, looked all about at the orderly, shipshape room that reflected her personality—as
did any room she occupied.

"Just the same," she called out, over her
shoulder, to Buck in the doorway, "I hate like
fury to see that order slide."

In hat and coat and furs she stood a moment,
her fingers on the electric switch, her eyes very
bright and wide. The memories of ten years,
fifteen years, twenty years crowded up around
her and filled the little room. Some of them

were golden and some of them were black; a few had power to frighten her, even now. So she turned out the light, stood for just another moment there in the darkness, then stepped out into the hall, closed the door softly behind her, and stood face to face with the lettering on the glass panel of the door—the lettering that spelled the name, "MRS. MCCHESNEY."

T. A. Buck watched her in silence. She reached up with one wavering forefinger and touched each of the twelve letters, one after the other. Then she spread her hand wide, blotting out the second word. And when she turned away, one saw—she being Emma McChesney, and a woman, and very tired and rather sentimental, and a bit hysterical and altogether happy—that, though she was smiling, her eyes were wet.

In her ten years on the road, visiting town after town, catching trains, jolting about in rumbling hotel 'buses or musty-smelling small-town hacks, living in hotels, good, bad, and indifferent, Emma McChesney had come upon hundreds of rice-strewn, ribbon-bedecked bridal couples. She had leaned from her window at many a railway station to see the barbaric and cruel old custom of bride-and-bridegroom baiting. She had smiled very tenderly—and rather sadly, and hopefully, too—upon the boy and girl who rushed breathless into the car in a flurry of white streamers, flowers, old shoes, laughter, cheers, last messages. Now, as in a dream, she found herself actually of these. Of rice, old shoes, and badinage there had been none, it is true. She stood quietly by while Buck attended to their trunks, just as she had seen it done by hundreds of helpless little cotton-wool women who had never checked a trunk in their lives—she, who had spent ten years of her life wrestling with trunks and baggagemen and porters. Once there was some trifling mistake—Buck's fault. Emma, with her experience of the road, saw his error. She could have set him right with a word. It was on the tip of her tongue. By sheer force of will she withheld that word, fought back the almost overwhelming inclination to take things in hand, set them right. It was just an incident, almost trifling in itself. But its import was tremendous, for her conduct, that moment, shaped the happiness of their future life together.

Emma had said that there would be no rude awakenings for them, no startling shocks.

"There isn't a thing we don't know about each other," she had said. "We each know the other's weaknesses and strength. I hate the way you gnaw your mustache when you're troubled, and I think the fuss you make when the waiter pours your coffee without first having given you sugar and cream is the most absurd thing I've ever seen. But, then, I know how it annoys you to see me sitting with one slipper dangling from my toe, when I'm particularly comfortable and snug. You know how I like my eggs, and you think it's immoral. I suppose we're really set in our ways. It's going to be interesting to watch each other shift."

"Just the same," Buck said, "I didn't dream there was any woman living who could actually make a Pullman drawing-room look homelike."

"Any woman who has spent a fourth of her life in hotels and trains learns that trick. She has to. If she happens to be the sort that likes books and flowers and sewing, she carries some of each with her. And one book, one rose, and one piece of unfinished embroidery would make an oasis in the Sahara Desert look homelike."

A CLOSER CORPORATION

It was on the westbound train that they encountered Sam—Sam of the rolling eye, the genial grin, the deft hand. Sam was known to every hardened traveler as the porter *de luxe* of the road. Sam was a diplomat, a financier, and a rascal. He never forgot a face. He never forgave a meager tip. The passengers who traveled with him were at once his guests and his victims.

Therefore his, "Good evenin', Mis' McChesney, ma'am. Good even'! Well, it suh't'nly has been a long time sense Ah had the pleasuh of yoh presence as passengah, ma'am. Ah sure am——"

The slim, elegant figure of T. A. Buck appeared in the doorway. Sam's rolling eye became a thing on ball bearings. His teeth flashed startlingly white in the broadest of grins. He took Buck's hat, ran a finger under its inner band, and shook it very gently.

"What's the idea?" inquired Buck genially. "Are you a combination porter and prestidigitator?"

Sam chuckled his infectious negro chuckle.

"Well, no, sah! Ah wouldn' go's fah as t' say that, sah. But Ah hab been known to shake rice out of a gen'lman's ordinary, ever'-day, black derby hat."

"Get out!" laughed T. A. Buck, as Sam ducked.

"You may as well get used to it," smiled Emma, "because I'm known to every train-conductor, porter, hotel-clerk, chamber-maid, and bell-boy between here and the Great Lakes."

It was Sam who proved himself hero of the honeymoon, for he saved T. A. Buck from continuing his journey to Chicago brideless. Fifteen minutes earlier, Buck had gone to the buffet-car for a smoke. At Cleveland, Emma, looking out of the car window, saw a familiar figure pacing up and down the station platform. It was that dapper and important little Irishman, O'Malley, buyer for Gage & Fosdick, the greatest mail-order house in the world—O'Malley, whose letter T. A. Buck had answered; O'Malley, whose order meant thousands. He was on his way to New York, of course.

In that moment Mrs. T. A. Buck faded into the background and Emma McChesney rose up in her place. She snatched hat and coat and furs, put them on as she went down the long aisle, swung down the car steps, and flew down the platform to the unconscious O'Malley. He was smoking, all unconscious. The Fates had delivered him into her expert hands. She knew those kindly sisters of old, and she was the last to refuse their largesse.

"Mr. O'Malley!"

He wheeled.

"Mrs. McChesney!" He had just a charming trace of a brogue. His enemies said he assumed it. "Well, who was I thinkin' of but you a minute ago. What———"

"I'm on my way to Chicago. Saw you from the car window. You're on the New York train? I thought so. Tell me, you're surely seeing our man, aren't you?"

O'Malley's smiling face clouded. He was a temperamental Irishman—Ted O'Malley— with ideas on the deference due him and his great house.

"I'll tell you the truth, Mrs. McChesney. I had a letter from your Mr. Buck. It wasn't much of a letter to a man like me, representing a house like Gage & Fosdick. It said both heads of the firm would be out of town, and would I see the manager. Me—see the manager! Well, thinks I, if that's how important

[103]

they think my order, then they'll not get it—
that's all. I've never yet———"

"Dear Mr. O'Malley, please don't be offended. As a McChesney to an O'Malley, I
want to tell you that I've just been married."

"Married! God bless me—to———"

"To T. A. Buck, of course. He's on that
train. He———"

She turned toward the train. And as she
turned it began to move, ever so gently. At
the same moment there sped toward her, with
unbelievable swiftness, the figure of Sam the
porter, his eyes all whites. By one arm he
grasped her, and half carried, half jerked her
to the steps of the moving train, swung her up
to the steps like a bundle of rags, caught the
rail by a miracle, and stood, grinning and triumphant, gazing down at the panting O'Malley,
who was running alongside the train.

"Back in a week. Will you wait for us in
New York?" called Emma, her breath coming
fast. She was trembling, too, and laughing.

"Will I wait!" called back the puffing O'Malley, every bit of the Irish in him beaming from
his eyes. "I'll be there when you get back as
sure as your name's McBuck."

A CLOSER CORPORATION

From his pocket he took a round, silver Western dollar and, still running, tossed it to the toothy Sam. That peerless porter caught it, twirled it, kissed it, bowed, and grinned afresh as the train glided out of the shed.

Emma, flushed, smiling, flew up the aisle.

Buck, listening to her laughing, triumphant account of her hairbreadth, harum-scarum adventure, frowned before he smiled.

"Emma, how could you do it! At least, why didn't you send back for me first?"

Emma smiled a little tremulously.

"Don't be angry. You see, dear boy, I've only been your wife for a week. But I've been Featherloom petticoats for over fifteen years. It's a habit."

Just how strong and fixed a habit, she proved to herself a little more than a week later. It was the morning of their first breakfast in the new apartment. You would have thought, to see them over their coffee and eggs and rolls, that they had been breakfasting together thus for years—Annie was so at home in her new kitchen; the deft little maid, in her crisp white, fitted so perfectly into the picture. Perhaps the thing that T. A. Buck said, once the maid

[105]

left them alone, might have given an outsider the cue.

"You remind me of a sweetpea, Emma. One of those crisp, erect, golden-white, fresh, fragrant sweetpeas. I think it is the slenderest, sweetest, neatest, trimmest flower in the world, so delicately set on its stem, and yet so straight, so independent."

"T. A., you say such dear things to me!"

No; they had not been breakfasting together for years.

"I'm glad you're not one of those women that wears a frowsy, lacy, ribbony, what-do-you-call-'em — boudoir-cap — down to breakfast. They always make me think of uncombed hair. That's just one reason why I'm glad."

"And I'm glad," said Emma, looking at his clear eyes and steady hand and firm skin, "for a number of reasons. One of them is that you're not the sort of man who's a grouch at breakfast."

When he had hat and coat and stick in hand, and had kissed her good-by and reached the door and opened it, he came back again, as is the way of bridegrooms. But at last the door closed behind him.

A CLOSER CORPORATION

Emma sat there a moment, listening to his quick, light step down the corridor, to the opening of the lift door, to its metallic closing. She sat there, in the sunshiny dining-room, in her fresh, white morning gown. She picked up her newspaper, opened it; scanned it, put it down. For years, now, she had read her newspaper in little gulps on the way downtown in crowded subway or street-car. She could not accustom herself to this leisurely scanning of the pages. She rose, went to the window, came back to the table, stood there a moment, her eyes fixed on something far away.

The swinging door between dining-room and butler's pantry opened. Annie, in her neat blue-and-white stripes, stood before her.

"Shall it be steak or chops to-night, Mrs. Mc—Buck?"

Emma turned her head in Annie's direction —then her eyes. The two actions were distinct and separate.

"Steak or——" There was a little bewildered look in her eyes. Her mind had not yet focused on the question. "Steak—oh! Oh, yes, of course! Why—why, Annie"—and the splendid thousand-h.-p. mind brought itself down to the settling of this butter-churning, two-h.-p. question—"why, Annie, considering all things, I think we'll make it *filet* with mushrooms."

IV

BLUE SERGE

FOR ten years, Mrs. Emma McChesney's home had been a wardrode-trunk. She had taken her family life at second hand. Four nights out of the seven, her bed was "Lower Eight," and her breakfast, as many mornings, a cinder-strewn, lukewarm horror, taken *tête-à-tête* with a sleepy-eyed stranger and presided over by a white-coated, black-faced bandit, to whom a coffee-slopped saucer was a matter of course.

It had been her habit during those ten years on the road as traveling saleswoman for the T. A. Buck Featherloom Petticoat Company, to avoid the discomfort of the rapidly chilling car by slipping early into her berth. There, in kimono, if not in comfort, she would shut down the electric light with a snap, raise the shade, and, propped up on one elbow, watch the little towns go by. They had a wonderful fascination for her, those Middle Western towns, whose very names had a comfortable, home-like sound—Sandusky, Galesburg, Crawfords-ville, Appleton—very real towns, with very real people in them. Peering wistfully out through the dusk, she could get little intimate glimpses of the home life of these people as the night came on. In those modest frame houses near the station they need not trouble to pull down the shades as must their cautious city cousins. As the train slowed down, there could be had a glimpse of a matronly house-wife moving deftly about in the kitchen's warm-yellow glow, a man reading a paper in slip-pered, shirt-sleeved comfort, a pig-tailed girl at the piano, a woman with a baby in her arms, or a family group, perhaps, seated about the table, deep in an after-supper conclave. It had made her homeless as she was homesick.

Emma always liked that picture best. Her keen, imaginative mind could sense the scene, could actually follow the trend of the talk dur-ing this, the most genial, homely, soul-cheering hour of the day. The trifling events of the last twelve hours in schoolroom, in store, in office, in street, in kitchen loom up large as they are rehearsed in that magic, animated, cozy moment just before ma says, with a sigh:

"Well, folks, go on into the sitting-room. Me and Nellie've got to clear away."

Just silhouettes as the train flashed by—these small-town people—but very human, very enviable to Emma McChesney.

"They're real," she would say. "They're regular, three-meals-a-day people. I've been peeking in at their windows for ten years, and I've learned that it is in these towns that folks really live. The difference between life here and life in New York is the difference between area and depth. D'you see what I mean? In New York, they live by the mile, and here they live by the cubic foot. Well, I'd rather have one juicy, thick club-steak than a whole platterful of quarter-inch. It's the same idea."

To those of her business colleagues whose habit it was to lounge in the hotel window with sneering comment upon the small-town procession as it went by, Emma McChesney had been wont to say:

"Don't sneer at Main Street. When you come to think of it, isn't it true that Fifth Avenue, any bright winter afternoon between four and six, is only Main Street on a busy day multiplied by one thousand?"

Emma McChesney was not the sort of woman to rail at a fate that had placed her in the harness instead of in the carriage. But during all the long years of up-hill pull, from the time she started with a humble salary in the office of the T. A. Buck Featherloom Petticoat Company, through the years spent on the road, up to the very time when the crown of success came to her in the form of the secretaryship of the prosperous firm of T. A. Buck, there was a minor but fixed ambition in her heart. That same ambition is to be found deep down in the heart of every woman whose morning costume is a tailor suit, whose newspaper must be read in hurried snatches on the way downtown in crowded train or car, and to whom nine A.M. spells "Business."

"In fifteen years," Emma McChesney used to say, "I've never known what it is to loll in leisure. I've never had a chance to luxuriate. Sunday? To a working woman, Sunday is for the purpose of repairing the ravages of the other six days. By the time you've washed your brushes, mended your skirt-braid, darned your stockings and gloves, looked for gray hairs and crows'-feet, and skimmed the magazine section, it's Monday."

It was small wonder that Emma McChesney's leisure had been limited. In those busy years she had not only earned the living for herself and her boy; she had trained that boy into manhood and placed his foot on the first rung of business success. She had transformed the T. A. Buck Featherloom Petticoat Company from a placidly mediocre concern to a thriving, flourishing, nationally known institution. All this might have turned another woman's head. It only served to set Emma McChesney's more splendidly on her shoulders. Not too splendidly, however; for, with her marriage to her handsome business partner, T. A. Buck, that well-set, independent head was found to fit very cozily into the comfortable hollow formed by T. A. Buck's right arm.

"Emma," Buck had said, just before their marriage, "what is the arrangement to be after —after——"

"Just what it is now, I suppose," Emma had replied, "except that we'll come down to the office together."

[113]

He had regarded her thoughtfully for a long minute. Then, "Emma, for three months after our marriage will you try being just Mrs. T. A. Buck?"

"You mean no factory, no Featherlooms, no dictation, no business bothers!" Her voice was a rising scale of surprise.

"Just try it for three months, with the privilege of a lifetime, if you like it. But try it. I—I'd like to see you there when I leave, Emma. I'd like to have you there when I come home. I suppose I sound like a selfish Turk, but——"

"You sound like a regular husband," Emma McChesney had interrupted, "and I love you for it. Now listen, T. A. For three whole months I'm going to be what the yellow novels used to call a doll-wife. I'm going to meet you at the door every night with a rose in my hair. I shall wear pink things with lace ruffles on 'em. Don't you know that I've been longing to do just those things for years and years? I'm going to blossom out into a beauty. Watch me! I've never had time to study myself. I'll hold shades of yellow and green and flesh-color up to my face to see which brings out the right

[114]

tints. I'm going to gaze at myself through half-closed eyes to see which shade produces tawny lights in my hair. Ever since I can remember, I've been so busy that it has been a question of getting the best possible garments in the least possible time for the smallest possible sum. In that case, one gets blue serge. I've worn blue serge until it feels like a convict's uniform. I'm going to blossom out into fawn and green and mauve. I shall get evening dresses with only bead shoulder-straps. I'm going to shop. I've never really seen Fifth Avenue between eleven and one, when the real people come out. My views of it have been at nine A.M. when the office-workers are going to work, and at five-thirty when they are going home. I will now cease to observe the proletariat and mingle with the predatory. I'll probably go in for those tiffin things at the Plaza. If I do, I'll never be the same woman again."

Whereupon she paused with dramatic effect.

To all of which T. A. Buck had replied:

"Go as far as you like. Take fencing lessons, if you want to, or Sanskrit. You've been a queen bee for so many years that I think the rôle of drone will be a pleasant change. Let me shoulder the business worries for a while. You've borne them long enough."

"It's a bargain. For three months I shall do nothing more militant than to pick imaginary threads off your coat lapel and pout when you mention business. At the end of those three months we'll go into private session, compare notes, and determine whether the plan shall cease or become permanent. Shake hands on it."

They shook hands solemnly. As they did so, a faint shadow of doubt hovered far, far back in the depths of T. A. Buck's fine eyes. And a faint, inscrutable smile lurked in the corners of Emma's lips.

So it was that Emma McChesney, the alert, the capable, the brisk, the business-like, assumed the rôle of Mrs. T. A. Buck, the leisurely, the languid, the elegant. She, who formerly, at eleven in the morning, might have been seen bent on selling the best possible bill of spring Featherlooms to Joe Greenbaum, of Keokuk, Iowa, could now be found in a modiste's gray-and-raspberry *salon*, being draped and pinned and fitted. She, whose dynamic force once charged the entire office and factory with energy and efficiency, now distributed a tithe of that priceless vigor here, a tithe there, a tithe everywhere, and thus broke the very backbone of its power.

She had never been a woman to do things by halves. What she undertook to do she did thoroughly and whole-heartedly. This principle she applied to her new mode of life as rigidly as she had to the old.

That first month slipped magically by. Emma was too much a woman not to feel a certain exquisite pleasure in the selecting of delicate and becoming fabrics. There was a thrill of novelty in being able to spend an hour curled up with a book after lunch, to listen to music one afternoon a week, to drive through the mistily gray park; to walk up the thronged, sparkling Avenue, pausing before its Aladdin's Cave windows. Simple enough pleasures, and taken quite as a matter of course by thousands of other women who had no work-filled life behind them to use as contrast.

She plunged into her new life whole-heartedly. The first new gown was exciting. It was a velvet affair with furs, and gratifyingly becoming. Her shining blond head rose above the

soft background of velvet and fur with an effect to distract the least observing.

"Like it?" she had asked Buck, turning
slowly, frankly sure of herself.

"You're wonderful in it," said T. A. Buck.
"Say, Emma, where's that blue thing you used
to wear—the one with the white cuffs and collar, and the little blue hat with the what-cha-
ma-call-ems on it?"

"T. A. Buck, you're—you're—well, you're
a man, that's what you are! That blue thing
was worn threadbare in the office, and I gave
it to the laundress's niece weeks ago." Small
wonder her cheeks took on a deeper pink.

"Oh," said Buck, unruffled, "too bad! There
was something about that dress—I don't
know——"

At the first sitting of the second gown,
Emma revolted openly.

On the floor at Emma's feet there was knot-
ted into a contortionistic attitude a small, wiry,
impolite person named Smalley. Miss Smalley
was an artist in draping and knew it. She was
the least fashionable person in all that smart
dressmaking establishment. She refused to notice the corset-coiffure-and-charmeuse edict that

[118]

governed all other employees in the shop. In her shabby little dress, her steel-rimmed spectacles, her black-sateen apron, Smalley might have passed for a Bird Center home dressmaker. Yet, given a yard or two or three of satin and a saucer of pins, Smalley could make the dumpiest of débutantes look like a fragile flower.

At a critical moment Emma stirred. Handicapped as she was by a mouthful of nineteen pins and her bow-knot attitude, Smalley still could voice a protest.

"Don't move!" she commanded, thickly.

"Wait a minute," Emma said, and moved again, more disastrously than before. "Don't you think it's too—too young?"

She eyed herself in the mirror anxiously, then looked down at Miss Smalley's nut-cracker face that was peering up at her, its lips pursed grotesquely over the pins.

"Of course it is," mumbled Miss Smalley. "Everybody's clothes are too young for 'em nowadays. The only difference between the dresses we make for girls of sixteen and the dresses we make for their grandmothers of sixty is that the sixty-year-old ones want 'em

shorter and lower, and they run more to rose-
bud trimming."

Emma surveyed the acid Miss Smalley with
a look that was half amused, half vexed, wholly
determined.

"I shan't wear it. Heaven knows I'm not
sixty, but I'm not sixteen either! I don't want
to be."

Miss Smalley, doubling again to her task,
flung upward a grudging compliment.

"Well, anyway, you've got the hair and the
coloring and the figure for it. Goodness knows
you look young enough!"

"That's because I've worked hard all my
life," retorted Emma, almost viciously. "Another month of this leisure and I'll be as wrinkled as the rest of them."

Smalley's magic fingers paused in their ma-
nipulation of a soft fold of satin.

"Worked? Earned a living? Used your
wits and brains every day against the wits and
brains of other folks?"

"Every day."

Into the eyes of Miss Smalley, the artist in
draping, there crept the shrewd twinkle of Miss
Smalley, the successful woman in business. She

had been sitting back on her knees, surveying her handiwork through narrowed lids. Now she turned her gaze on Emma, who was smiling down at her.

"Then for goodness' sake don't stop! I've found out that work is a kind of self-oiler. If you're used to it, the minute you stop you begin to get rusty, and your hinges creak and you clog up. And the next thing you know, you break down. Work that you like to do is a blessing. It keeps you young. When my mother was my age, she was crippled with rheumatism, and all gnarled up, and quavery, and all she had to look forward to was death. Now me—every time the styles in skirts change I get a new hold on life. And on a day when I can make a short, fat woman look like a tall, thin woman, just by sitting here on my knees with a handful of pins, and giving her the line she needs, I go home feeling like I'd just been born."

"I know that feeling," said Emma, in her eyes a sparkle that had long been absent. "I've had it when I've landed a thousand-dollar Featherloom order from a man who has assured me that he isn't interested in our line."

[121]

At dinner that evening, Emma's gown was so obviously not of the new crop that even her husband's inexpert eye noted it.

"That's not one of the new ones, is it?"

"This! And you a manufacturer of skirts!"

"What's the matter with the supply of new dresses? Isn't there enough to go round?"

"Enough! I've never had so many new gowns in my life. The trouble is that I shan't feel at home in them until I've had 'em all dry-cleaned at least once."

During the second month, there came a sudden, sharp change in skirt modes. For four years women had been mincing along in garments so absurdly narrow that each step was a thing to be considered, each curbing or car-step demanding careful negotiation. Now, Fashion, in her freakiest mood, commanded a bewildering width of skirt that was just one remove from the flaring hoops of Civil War days. Emma knew what that meant for the Featherloom workrooms and selling staff. New designs, new models, a shift in prices, a boom for petticoats, for four years a garment despised.

A hundred questions were on the tip of Emma's tongue; a hundred suggestions flashed into her keen mind; there occurred to her a wonderful design for a new model which should be full and flaring without being bulky and uncomfortable as were the wide petticoats of the old days.

But a bargain was a bargain. Still, Emma Buck was as human as Emma McChesney had been. She could not resist a timid,

"T. A., are you—that is—I was just wondering—you're making 'em wide, I suppose, for the spring trade."

A queer look flashed into T. A. Buck's eyes —a relieved look that was as quickly replaced by an expression both baffled and anxious.

"Why—a—mmmm—yes—oh, yes, we're making 'em up wide, but——"

"But what?" Emma leaned forward, tense.

"Oh, nothing—nothing."

During the second month there came calling on Emma, those solid and heavy New Yorkers, with whom the Buck family had been on friendly terms for many years. They came at the correct hour, in their correct motor or conservative broughams, wearing their quietly correct clothes, and Emma gave them tea, and they talked on every subject from suffrage to salad dressings, and from war to weather, but never once was mention made of business. And Emma McChesney's life had been interwoven with business for more than fifteen years.

There were dinners—long, heavy, correct dinners. Emma, very well dressed, bright-eyed, alert, intelligent, vital, became very popular at these affairs, and her husband very proud of her popularity. And if any one as thoroughly alive as Mrs. T. A. Buck could have been bored to extinction by anything, then those dinners would have accomplished the deadly work.

"T. A.," she said one evening, after a particularly large affair of this sort, "T. A., have you ever noticed anything about me that is different from other women?"

"Have I? Well, I should say I——"

"Oh, I don't mean what you mean, dear—thanks just the same. I mean those women tonight. They all seem to 'go in' for something —votes or charity or dancing or social service, or something—even the girls. And they all sounded so amateurish, so untrained, so unprepared, yet they seemed to be dreadfully in earnest."

"This is the difference," said T. A. Buck.

"You've rubbed up against life, and you know. They've always been sheltered, but now they want to know. Well, naturally they're going to bungle and bump their heads a good many times before they really find out."

"Anyway," retorted Emma, "they want to know. That's something. It's better to have bumped your head, even though you never see what's on the other side of the wall, than never to have tried to climb it."

It was in the third week of the third month that Emma encountered Hortense. Hortense, before her marriage to Henry, the shipping-clerk, had been a very pretty, very pert, very devoted little stenographer in the office of the T. A. Buck Featherloom Petticoat Company. She had married just a month after her employers, and Emma, from the fulness of her own brimming cup of happiness, had made Hortense happy with a gift of linens and lingerie and lace of a fineness that Hortense's beauty-loving, feminine heart could never have hoped for.

They met in the busy aisle of a downtown department store and shook hands as do those who have a common bond.

Hortense, as pretty as ever and as pert, spoke first.

"I wouldn't have known you, Mrs. Mc— Buck!"

"No? Why not?"

"You look—no one would think you'd ever worked in your life. I was down at the office the other day for a minute—the first time since I was married. They told me you weren't there any more."

"No; I haven't been down since my marriage either. I'm like you—an elegant lady of leisure."

Hortense's bright-blue eyes dwelt searchingly on the face of her former employer.

"The bunch in the office said they missed you something awful." Then, in haste: "Oh, I don't mean that Mr. Buck don't make things go all right. They're awful fond of him. But— I don't know—Miss Kelly said she never has got over waiting for the sound of your step down the hall at nine—sort of light and quick and sharp and busy, as if you couldn't wait till you waded into the day's work. Do you know what I mean?"

"I know what you mean," said Emma.

" 'No; I'm like you—an elegant lady of leisure' "—*Page 126*

There was a little pause. The two women so far apart, yet so near; so different, yet so like, gazed far down into each other's soul.

"Miss it, don't you?" said Hortense.

"Yes; don't you?"

"Do I! Say——" She turned and indicated the women surging up and down the store aisles, and her glance and gesture were replete with contempt. "Say; look at 'em! Wandering around here, aimless as a lot of chickens in a barnyard. Half of 'em are here because they haven't got anything else to do. Think of it! I've watched 'em lots of times. They go pawing over silks and laces and trimmings just for the pleasure of feeling 'em. They stand in front of a glass case with a figure in it all dressed up in satin and furs and jewels, and you'd think they were worshiping an idol like they used to in the olden days. They don't seem to have anything to do. Nothing to occupy their—their heads. Say, if I thought I was going to be like them in time, I——"

"Hortense, my dear child, you're—you're happy, aren't you? Henry——"

"Well, I should say we are! I'm crazy about Henry, and he thinks I'm perfect. Hon-

estly, ain't they a scream! They think they're
so big and manly and all, and they're just like
kids; ain't it so? We're living in a four-room
apartment in Harlem. We've got it fixed up
too cozy for anything."

"I'd like to come and see you," said Emma.
Hortense opened her eyes wide.

"Honestly; if you would——"

"Let's go up now. I've the car outside."

"Now! Why I—I'd love it!"

They chattered like schoolgirls on the way
uptown——these two who had found so much
in common. The little apartment reached,
Hortense threw open the door with the confident gesture of the housekeeper who is not
afraid to have her household taken by surprise
—whose housekeeping is an index of character.

Hortense had been a clean-cut little stenographer. Her correspondence had always been
free from erasures, thumb-marks, errors. Her
four-room flat was as spotless as her typewritten letters had been. The kitchen shone in its
blue and white and nickel. A canary chirped
in the tiny dining-room. There were books
and magazines on the sitting-room table. The
bedroom was brave in its snowy spread and

the toilet silver that had been Henry's gift to her the Christmas they became engaged.

Emma examined everything, exclaimed over everything, admired everything. Hortense glowed like a rose.

"Do you really like it? I like the green velours in the sitting-room, don't you? It's always so kind and cheerful. We're not all settled yet. I don't suppose we ever will be. Sundays, Henry putters around, putting up shelves, and fooling around with a can of paint. I always tell him he ought to have lived on a farm, where he'd have elbow-room."

"No wonder you're so happy and busy," Emma exclaimed, and patted the girl's fresh, young cheek.

Hortense was silent a moment.

"I'm happy," she said, at last, "but I ain't busy. And—well, if you're not busy, you can't be happy very long, can you?"

"No," said Emma, "idleness, when you're not used to it, is misery."

"There! You've said it! It's like running on half-time when you're used to a day-and-night shift. Something's lacking. It isn't that Henry isn't grand to me, because he is. Evenings, we're so happy that we just sit and grin at each other and half the time we forget to go to a 'movie.' After Henry leaves in the morning, I get to work. I suppose, in the old days, when women used to have to chop the kindling, and catch the water for washing in a rain-barrel, and keep up a fire in the kitchen stove and do their own bread baking and all, it used to keep 'em hustling. But, my goodness! A four-room flat for two isn't any work. By eleven, I'm through. I've straightened everything, from the bed to the refrigerator; the marketing's done, and the dinner vegetables are sitting around in cold water. The mending for two is a joke. Henry says it's a wonder I don't sew double-breasted buttons on his undershirts."

Emma was not smiling. But, then, neither was Hortense. She was talking lightly, seemingly, but her pretty face was quite serious.

"The big noise in my day is when Henry comes home at six. That was all right and natural, I suppose, in those times when a quilting-bee was a wild afternoon's work, and teaching school was the most advanced job a woman could hold down."

BLUE SERGE

Emma was gazing fascinated at the girl's sparkling face. Her own eyes were very bright, and her lips were parted.

"Tell me, Hortense," she said now; "what does Henry say to all this? Have you told him how you feel?"

"Well, I—I talked to him about it once or twice. I told him that I've got about twenty-four solid hours a week that I might be getting fifty cents an hour for. You know, I worked for a manuscript-typewriting concern before I came over to Buck's—plays and stories and that kind of thing. They used to like my work because I never queered their speeches by leaving out punctuation or mixing up the characters. The manager there said I could have work any time I wanted it. I've got my own typewriter. I got it second hand when I first started in. Henry picks around on it sometimes, evenings. I hardly ever touch it. It's getting rusty—and so am I."

"It isn't just the money you want, Hortense? Are you sure?"

"Of course I'd like the money. That extra coming in would mean books—I'm crazy about reading, and so is Henry—and theaters and lots of things we can't afford now. But that isn't all. Henry don't want to be a shipping-clerk all his life. He's crazy about mechanics and that kind of stuff. But the books that he needs cost a lot. Don't you suppose I'd be proud to feel that the extra money I'd earned would lift him up where he could have a chance to be something! But Henry is dead set against it. He says he is the one that's going to earn the money around here. I try to tell him that I'm used to using my mind. He laughs and pinches my cheek and tells me to use it thinking about him." She stopped suddenly and regarded Emma with conscience-stricken eyes. "You don't think I'm running down Henry, do you? My goodness, I don't want you to think that I'd change back again for a million dollars, because I wouldn't."

She looked up at Emma, conscience-stricken.

Emma came swiftly over and put one hand on the girl's shoulder.

"I don't think it. Not for a minute. I know that the world is full of Henrys, and that the number of Hortenses is growing larger and larger. I don't know if the four-room flats are to blame, or whether it's just a natural development. But the Henry-Hortense situation seems to be spreading to the nine-room-and-three-baths apartments, too."

Hortense nodded a knowing head.

"I kind of thought so, from the way you were listening."

The two, standing there gazing at each other almost shyly, suddenly began to laugh. The laugh was a safety-valve. Then, quite as suddenly, both became serious. That seriousness had been the under-current throughout.

"I wonder," said Emma very gently, "if a small Henry, some day, won't provide you with an outlet for all that stored-up energy."

Hortense looked up very bravely.

"Maybe. You—you must have been about my age when your boy was born. Did he make you feel—different?"

The shade of sadness that always came at the mention of those unhappy years of her early marriage crept into Emma's face now.

"That was not the same, dear," she explained. "I hadn't your sort of Henry. You see, my boy was my only excuse for living. You'll never know what that means. And when things grew altogether impossible, and I knew

[133]

that I must earn a living for Jock and myself, I just did it—that's all. I had to."

Hortense thought that over for one deliberate moment. Her brows were drawn in a frown.

"I'll tell you what I think," she announced, at last, "though I don't know that I can just exactly put it into words. I mean this: Some people are just bound to—to give, to build up things, to—well, to manufacture, because they just can't help it. It's in 'em, and it's got to come out. Dynamos—that's what Henry's technical books would call them. You're one— a great big one. I'm one. Just a little tiny one. But it's sparking away there all the time, and it might as well be put to some use, mightn't it?"

Emma bent down and kissed the troubled forehead, and then, very tenderly, the pretty, puckered lips.

"Little Hortense," she said, "you're asking a great big question. I can answer it for myself, but I can't answer it for you. It's too dangerous. I wouldn't if I could."

Emma, waiting in the hall for the lift, looked back at the slim little figure in the doorway.

There was a droop to the shoulders. Emma's heart smote her.

"Don't bother your head about all this, little girl," she called back to her. "Just forget to be ambitious and remember to be happy. That's much the better way."

Hortense, from the doorway, grinned a rather wicked little grin.

"When are you going back to the office, Mrs. Buck?" she asked, quietly enough.

"What makes you think I'm going back at all?" demanded Emma, stepping into the shaky little elevator.

"I don't think it," retorted Hortense, once more the pert. "I know it."

Emma knew it, too. She had known it from the moment that she shook hands in her compact. There was still one week remaining of the stipulated three months. It seemed to Emma that that one week was longer than the combined eleven. But she went through with colors flying. Whatever Emma McChesney Buck did, she did well. But, then, T. A. Buck had done his part well, too—so well that, on the final day, Emma felt a sinking at her heart. He seemed so satisfied with affairs as they were.

He was, apparently, so content to drop all thought of business when he left the office for his home.

Emma had planned a very special little dinner that evening. She wore a very special gown, too—one of the new ones. T. A. noticed it at once, and the dinner as well, being that kind of husband. Still, Annie, the cook, complained later, to the parlor-maid, about the thanklessness of cooking dinners for folks who didn't eat more'n a mouthful, anyway.

Dinner over,

"Well, Emma?" said T. A. Buck.

"Light your cigar, T. A.," said Emma. "You'll need it."

T. A. lighted it with admirable leisureliness, sent out a great puff of fragrant smoke, and surveyed his wife through half-closed lids. Beneath his air of ease there was a tension.

"Well, Emma?" he said again, gently.

Emma looked at him a moment appreciatively. She had too much poise and balance and control herself not to recognize and admire those qualities in others.

"T. A., if I had been what they call a homebody, we wouldn't be married to-day, would we?"

"No."

"You knew plenty of home-women that you could have married, didn't you?"

"I didn't ask them, Emma, but——"

"You know what I mean. Now listen, T. A.: I've loafed for three months. I've lolled and lazied and languished. And I've never been so tired in my life—not even when we were taking January inventory. Another month of this, and I'd be an old, old woman. I understand, now, what it is that brings that hard, tired, stony look into the faces of the idle women. They have to work so hard to try to keep happy. I suppose if I had been a homebody all my life, I might be hardened to this kind of thing. But it's too late now. And I'm thankful for it. Those women who want to shop and dress and drive and play are welcome to my share of it. If I am to be punished in the next world for my wickedness in this, I know what form my torture will take. I shall have to go from shop to shop with a piece of lace in my hand, matching a sample of insertion. Fifteen years of being in the thick of it spoil one for tatting and tea. The world is full of homebodies, I suppose. And they're happy. I suppose I might have been one, too, if I hadn't been obliged to get out and hustle. But it's too late to learn now. Besides, I don't want to. If I do try, I'll be destroying the very thing that attracted you to me in the first place. Remember what you said about the Fifth Avenue girl?"

"But, Emma," interrupted Buck very quietly, "I don't want you to try."

Emma, with a rush of words at her very lips, paused, eyed him for a doubtful moment, asked a faltering question.

"But it was your plan—you said you wanted me to be here when you came home and when you left, didn't you? Do you mean you——"

"I mean that I've missed my business partner every minute for three months. All the time we've been going to those fool dinners and all that kind of thing, I've been bursting to talk skirts to you. I—say, Emma, Adler's designed a new model—a full one, of course, but there's something wrong with it. I can't put my finger on the flaw, but——"

Emma came swiftly over to his chair.

"Make a sketch of it, can't you?" she said.

From his pocket Buck drew a pencil, an envelope, and fell to sketching rapidly, squinting down through his cigar smoke as he worked.

"It's like this," he began, absorbed and happy; "you see, where the fulness begins at the knee——"

"Yes!" prompted Emma, breathlessly.

Two hours later they were still bent over the much marked bit of paper. But their interest in it was not that of those who would solve a perplexing problem. It was the lingering, satisfied contemplation of a task accomplished.

Emma straightened, leaned back, sighed—a victorious, happy sigh.

"And to think," she said, marveling, "to think that I once envied the women who had nothing to do but the things I've done in the last three months!"

Buck had risen, stretched luxuriously, yawned. Now he came over to his wife and took her head in his two hands, cozily, and stood a moment looking into her shining eyes.

"Emma, I may have mentioned this once or twice before, but perhaps you'll still be interested to know that I think you're a wonder. A wonder! You're the——"

"Oh, well, we won't quarrel about that," smiled Emma brazenly. "But I wonder if Adler will agree with us when he sees what we've done to his newest skirt design."

Suddenly a new thought seemed to strike her. She was off down the hall. Buck, following in a leisurely manner, hands in pockets, stood in the bedroom door and watched her plunge into the innermost depths of the clothes-closet.

"What's the idea, Emma?"

"Looking for something," came back his wife's muffled tones.

A long wait.

"Can I help?"

"I've got it!" cried Emma, and emerged triumphant, flushed, smiling, holding a garment at arm's length, aloft.

"What——"

Emma shook it smartly, turned it this way and that, held it up under her chin by the sleeves.

"Why, girl!" exclaimed Buck, all a-grin, "it's the——"

"The blue serge," Emma finished for him,

[140]

"with the white collars and cuffs. And what's more, young man, it's the little blue hat with the what-cha-ma-call-ems on it. And praise be! I'm wearing 'em both down-town to-morrow morning."

V

"HOOPS, MY DEAR!"

EMMA McCHESNEY BUCK always
vigorously disclaimed any knowledge of
that dreamy-eyed damsel known as Inspiration.
T. A. Buck, her husband-partner, accused her
of being on intimate terms with the lady. So
did the adoring office staff of the T. A. Buck
Featherloom Petticoat Company. Out in the
workshop itself, the designers and cutters, those
jealous artists of the pencil, shears, and yard-
stick, looked on in awed admiration on those
rare occasions when the feminine member of
the business took the scissors in her firm white
hands and slashed boldly into a shimmering
length of petticoat-silk. When she put down
the great shears, there lay on the table the detached parts of that which the appreciative and
experienced eyes of the craftsmen knew to be a
new and original variation of that elastic garment known as the underskirt.

"HOOPS, MY DEAR!"

For weeks preceding one of these cutting-exhibitions, Emma was likely to be not quite her usual brisk self. A mystic glow replaced the alert brightness of her eye. Her wide-awake manner gave way to one of almost sluggish inactivity.

The outer office, noting these things, would lift its eyebrows significantly.

"Another hunch!" it would whisper. "The last time she beat the rest of the trade by six weeks with that elastic-top gusset."

"Inspiration working, Emma?" T. A. Buck would ask, noting the symptoms.

"It isn't inspiration, T. A. Nothing of the kind! It's just an attack of imagination, complicated by clothes-instinct."

"That's all that ails Poiret," Buck would retort.

Early in the autumn, when women were still walking with an absurd sidewise gait, like a duck, or a filly that is too tightly hobbled, the junior partner of the firm began to show unmistakable signs of business aberration. A blight seemed to have fallen upon her bright little office, usually humming with activity. The machinery of her day, ordinarily as noiseless and well ordered as a thing on ball bearings, now rasped, creaked, jerked, stood still, jolted on again. A bustling clerk or stenographer, entering with paper or memorandum, would find her bent over her desk, pencil in hand, absorbed in a rough drawing that seemed to bear no relation to the skirt of the day. The margin of her morning paper was filled with queer little scrawls by the time she reached the office. She drew weird lines with her fork on the table-cloth at lunch. These hieroglyphics she covered with a quick hand, like a bashful schoolgirl, when any one peeped.

"Tell a fellow what it's going to be, can't you?" pleaded Buck. "I got one glimpse yesterday, when you didn't know I was looking over your shoulder. It seemed a pass between an overgrown Zeppelin and an apple dumpling. So I know it can't be a skirt. Come on, Emma; tell your old man!"

"Not yet," Emma would reply dreamily.

Buck would strike an attitude intended to intimidate.

"If you have no sense of what is due me as your husband, then I demand, as senior partner of this firm, to know what it is that is taking your time, which rightfully belongs to this business."

"Go away, T. A., and stop pestering me! What do you think I'm designing—a doily?"

Buck, turning to go to his own office, threw a last retort over his shoulder—a rather sobering one, this time.

"Whatever it is, it had better be good—with business what it is and skirts what they are."

Emma lifted her head to reply to that.

"It isn't what they are that interests me. It's what they're going to be."

Buck paused in the doorway.

"Going to be! Anybody can see that. Underneath that full, fool, flaring over-drape, the real skirt is as tight as ever. I don't think the spring models will show an inch of real difference. I tell you, Emma, it's serious."

Emma, apparently absorbed in her work, did not reply to this. But a vague something about the back of her head told T. A. Buck that she was laughing at him. The knowledge only gave him new confidence in this resourceful, many-sided, lovable, level-headed partner-wife of his.

Two weeks went by—four—six—eight.

Emma began to look a little thin. Her bright color was there only when she was overtired or excited. The workrooms began to talk of new designs for spring, though it was scarcely midwinter. The head designer came forward timidly with a skirt that measured a yard around the bottom. Emma looked at it, tried to keep her lower lip prisoner between her teeth, failed, and began to laugh helplessly, almost hysterically.

Amazement in the faces of Buck and Koritz, the designer, became consternation, then, in the designer, resentment.

Koritz, dark, undersized, with the eyes of an Oriental and the lean, sensitive fingers of one who creates, shivered a little, like a plant that is swept by an icy blast. Buck came over and laid one hand on his wife's shaking shoulder.

"Emma, you're overtired! This—this thing you've been slaving over has been too much for you."

With one hand, Emma reached up and patted the fingers that rested protectingly on her shoulder. With the other, she wiped her eyes, then, all contrition, grasped the slender brown hand of the offended Koritz.

"Bennie, please forgive me! I—I didn't mean to laugh. I wasn't laughing at your new skirt."

"You think it's too wide, maybe, huh?" Bennie Koritz said, and held it up doubtfully.

"Too wide!" For a moment Emma seemed threatened with another attack of that inexplicable laughter. She choked it back resolutely.

"No, Bennie; not too wide. I'll tell you tomorrow why I laughed. Then, perhaps, you'll laugh with me."

Bennie, draping his despised skirt-model over one arm, had the courage to smile even now, though grimly.

"I laugh—sure," he said, showing his white teeth now. "But the laugh will be, I bet you, on me—like it was when you designed that knickerbocker before the trade knew such a thing could be."

Impulsively Emma grasped his hand and shook it, as though she found a certain needed encouragement in the loyalty of this sallow little Russian.

"Bennie, you're a true artist—because you're big enough to praise the work of a fel-

[147]

low craftsman when you recognize its value."

And Koritz, the dull red showing under the olive of his cheeks, went back to his cutting-table happy.

Buck bent forward, eagerly.

"You're going to tell me now, Emma? It's finished?"

"To-night—at home. I want to be the first to try it on. I'll play model. A private exhibition, just for you. It's not only finished; it is patented."

"Patented! But why? What is it, anyway? A new fastener? I thought it was a skirt."

"Wait until you see it. You'll think I should have had it copyrighted as well, not to say passed by the national board of censors."

"Do you mean to say that I'm to be the entire audience at the *première* of this new model?"

"You are to be audience, critic, orchestra, box-holder, patron, and 'Diamond Jim' Brady. Now run along into your own office—won't you, dear? I want to get out these letters." And she pressed the button that summoned a stenographer.

"'Do you mean to say that I'm to be the entire audience at the *première* of this new model?'"—*Page 148*

"HOOPS, MY DEAR!"

T. A. Buck, resigned, admiring, and antici-patory, went.

Annie, the cook, was justified that evening in her bitter complaint. Her excellent dinner received scant enough attention from these two. They hurried through it like eager, bright-eyed school-children who have been promised a treat. Two scarlet spots glowed in Emma's cheeks. Buck's eyes, through the haze of his after-dinner cigar, were luminous.

"Now?"

"No; not yet. I want you to smoke your cigar and digest your dinner and read your paper. I want you to twiddle your thumbs a little and look at your watch. First-night curtains are always late in rising, aren't they? Well!"

She turned on the full glare of the chandelier, turned it off, went about flicking on the soft-shaded wall lights and the lamps.

"Turn your chair so that your back will be toward the door."

He turned it obediently.

Emma vanished.

From the direction of her bedroom there presently came the sounds of dresser drawers hurriedly opened and shut with a bang, of a slipper dropped on the hard-wood floor, a tune hummed in an absent-minded absorption under the breath, an excited little laugh nervously stifled. Buck, in his rôle of audience, began to clap impatiently and to stamp with his feet on the floor.

"No gallery!" Emma called in from the hall. "Remember the temperamental family on the floor below!" A silence—then: "I'm coming. Shut your eyes and prepare to be jarred by the Buck balloon-petticoat!"

There was a rustling of silks, a little rush to the center of the big room, a breathless pause, a sharp snap of finger and thumb. Buck opened his eyes.

He opened his eyes. Then he closed them and opened them again, quickly, as we do, sometimes, when we are unwilling to believe that which we see. What he beheld was this: A very pretty, very flushed, very bright-eyed woman, her blond hair dressed quaintly after the fashion of the early 'Sixties, her arms and shoulders bare, a pink-slip with shoulder-straps in lieu of a bodice, and—he passed a bewildered hand over his eyes—a skirt that billowed and flared and flounced and spread in a great, graceful circle—a skirt strangely light for all its fulness—a skirt like, and yet, somehow, un-like those garments seen in ancient copies of *Godey's Lady Book.*

"That can't be—you don't mean—what—what *is* it?" stammered Buck, dismayed.

Emma, her arms curved above her head like a ballet-dancer's, pirouetted, curtsied very low so that the skirt spread all about her on the floor, like the petals of a flower.

"Hoops, my dear!"

"Hoops!" echoed Buck, in weak protest. "Hoops, my *dear!*"

Emma stroked one silken fold with approv-ing fingers.

"Our new leader for spring."

"But, Emma, you're joking!"

She stared, suddenly serious.

"You mean—you don't like it!"

"Like it! For a fancy-dress costume, yes; but as a petticoat for every-day wear, to be made up by us for our customers! But of course you're playing a trick on me." He laughed a little weakly and came toward her. "You can't catch me that way, old girl! It's darned becoming, Emma—I'll say that." He bent down, smiling. "I'll allow you to kiss me. And then try me with the real surprise, will you?"

Her coquetry vanished. Her smile fled with it. Her pretty pose was abandoned. Mrs. T. A. Buck, wife, gave way to Emma McChesney Buck, business woman. She stiffened a little, as though bracing herself for a verbal encounter.

"You'll get used to it. I expected you to be jolted at the first shock of it. I was, myself—when the idea came to me."

Buck passed a frenzied forefinger under his collar, as though it had suddenly grown too tight for him.

"Used to it! I don't want to get used to it! It's preposterous! You can't be serious! No woman would wear a garment like that! For five years skirts have been tighter and tighter——"

"Until this summer they became tightest," interrupted Emma. "They could go no farther. I knew that meant, 'About face!' I knew it meant not a slightly wider skirt but a wildly wider skirt. A skirt as bouffant as the other

[152]

had been scant. I was sure it wouldn't be a gradual process at all but a mushroom growth —hobbles to-day, hoops to-morrow. Study the history of women's clothes, and you'll find that has always been true."

"Look here, Emma," began Buck, desperately; "you're wrong, all wrong! Here, let me throw this scarf over your shoulders. Now we'll sit down and talk this thing over sensibly."

"I'll agree to the scarf"—she drew a soft, silken, fringed shawl about her and immediately one thought of a certain vivid, brilliant portrait of a hoop-skirted dancer—"but don't ask me to sit down. I'd rebound like a toy balloon. I've got to convince you of this thing. I'll have to do it standing."

Buck sank into his chair and dabbed at his forehead with his handkerchief.

"You'll never convince me, sitting or standing. Emma, I know I fought the knickerbocker when you originated it, and I know that it turned out to be a magnificent success. But this is different. The knicker was practical; this thing's absurd—it's impossible! This is an age of activity. In Civil War days women minced daintily along when they walked at all. They stitched on samplers by way of diversion."

"What has all that to do with it?" inquired Emma sweetly.

"Everything. Use a little logic."

"Logic! In a discussion about women's dress! T. A., I'm surprised."

"But, Emma, be reasonable. Good Lord! You're usually clear-sighted enough. Our mode of living has changed in the last fifty years— our methods of transit, our pastimes, customs, everything. Imagine a woman trying to climb a Fifth Avenue 'bus in one of those things. Fancy her in a hot set of tennis. Women use street-cars, automobiles, airships. Can you see a subway train full of hoop-skirted clerks, stenographers, and models? Street-car steps aren't built for it. Office-building elevators can't stand for it. Six-room apartments won't accommodate 'em. They're fantastic, wild, improbable. You're wrong, Emma—all wrong!"

She had listened patiently enough, never once attempting to interrupt. But on her lips was the maddening half-smile of one whose rebuttal is ready. Now she perched for a moment at the extreme edge of the arm of a chair. Her

[154]

skirt subsided decorously. Buck noticed that, with surprise, even in the midst of his heated protest.

"T. A., you've probably forgotten, but those are the very arguments used when the hobble was introduced. Preposterous, people said— impossible! Women couldn't walk in 'em. Wouldn't, couldn't sit down in 'em. Women couldn't run, play tennis, skate in them. The car steps were too high for them. Well, what happened? Women had to walk in them, and a new gait became the fashion. Women took lessons in how to sit down in them. They slashed them for tennis and skating. And street-car companies all over the country lowered the car steps to accommodate them. What's true for the hobble holds good for the hoop. Women will cease to single-foot and learn to undulate when they walk. They'll widen the car platforms. They'll sit on top the Fifth Avenue 'buses, and you'll never give them a second thought."

"The things don't stay where they belong. I've seen 'em misbehave in musical comedies," argued Buck miserably.

"That's where my patent comes in. The

old hoop was cumbersome, unwieldy, clumsy. The new skirt, by my patent featherboning process, is made light, graceful, easily managed. T. A., I predict that by midsummer a tight skirt will be as rare a sight as a full one was a year ago."

"Nonsense!"

"We're not quarreling, are we?"

"Quarreling! I rather think not! A man can have his own opinion, can't he?"

It appeared, however, that he could not. For when they had threshed it out, inch by inch, as might two partners whose only bond was business, it was Emma who won.

"Remember, I'm not convinced," Buck warned her; "I'm only beaten by superior force. But I do believe in your woman's intuition—I'll say that. It has never gone wrong. I'm banking on it."

"It's woman's intuition when we win," Emma observed, thoughtfully. "When we lose it's a foolish, feminine notion."

There were to be no half-way measures. The skirt was to be the feature of the spring line. Cutters and designers were one with Buck in thinking it a freak garment. Emma reminded them that the same thing had been said of the hobble on its appearance.

In February, Billy Spalding, veteran skirt-salesman, led a flying wedge of six on a test-trip that included the Middle West and the Coast. Their sample-trunks had to be rebuilt to accommodate the new model. Spalding, shirt-sleeved, whistling dolorously, eyed each garment with a look of bristling antagonism. Spalding sold skirts on commission.

Emma, surveying his labors, lifted a quizzical eyebrow.

"If you're going to sell that skirt as enthusiastically as you pack it, you'd better stay here in New York and save the house traveling expenses."

Spalding ceased to whistle. He held up a billowy sample and gazed at it.

"Honestly, Mrs. Buck, you know I'd try to sell pretzels in London if you asked me to. But do you really think any woman alive would be caught wearing a garment like this in these days?"

"Not only do I think it, Billy; I'm certain of it. This new petticoat makes me the Lincoln of the skirt trade. I'm literally freeing my sisters from the shackles that have bound their ankles for five years."

Spalding, unimpressed, folded another skirt.

"Um, maybe! But what's that line about slaves hugging their chains?"

The day following, Spalding and his flying squad scattered to spread the light among the skirt trade. And things went wrong from the start.

The first week showed an ominous lack of those cheering epistles beginning, "Enclosed please find," etc. The second was worse. The third was equally bad. The fourth was final. The second week in March, Spalding returned from a territory which had always been known as firmly wedded to the T. A. Buck Feather-loom petticoat. The Middle West would have none of him.

They held the post-mortem in Emma's bright little office, and that lady herself seemed to be strangely sunny and undaunted, considering the completeness of her defeat. She sat at her desk now, very interested, very bright-eyed, very calm. Buck, in a chair at the side of her desk, was interested, too, but not so calm. Spalding, who was accustomed to talk while standing,

leaned against the desk, feet crossed, brows fur-
rowed. As he talked, he emphasized his re-
marks by jabbing the air with his pencil.

"Well," said Emma quietly, "it didn't go."

"It didn't even start," corrected Spalding.

"But why?" demanded Buck. "Why?"

Spalding leaned forward a little, eagerly.

"I'll tell you something: When I started out
with that little garment, I thought it was a joke.
Before I'd been out with it a week, I began to
like it. In ten days, I was crazy about it, and
I believed in it from the waistband to the hem.
On the level, Mrs. Buck, I think it's a wonder.
Now, can you explain that?"

"Yes," said Emma; "you didn't like it at
first because it was a shock to you. It outraged
all your ideas of what a skirt ought to be.
Then you grew accustomed to it. Then you began to see its good points. Why couldn't you
make the trade get your viewpoint?"

"This is why: Out in Manistee and Oshkosh and Terre Haute, the girls have just really
learned the trick of walking in tight skirts. It's
as impossible to convince a Middle West buyer
that the exaggerated full skirt is going to be
worn next summer as it would be to prove to

him that men are going to wear sunbonnets. They thought I was trying to sell 'em masquerade costumes. I may believe in it, and you may believe in it, and T. A.; but the girls from Joplin—well, they're from Joplin. And they're waiting to hear from headquarters."

T. A. Buck crossed one leg over the other and sat up with a little sigh.

"Well, that settles it, doesn't it?" he said.

"It does not," replied Emma McChesney Buck crisply. "If they want to hear from headquarters, they won't have long to wait."

"Now, Emma, don't try to push this thing if it——"

"T. A., please don't look so forgiving. I'd much rather have you reproach me."

"It's you I'm thinking of, not the skirt."

"But I want you to think of the skirt, too. We've gone into this thing, and it has cost us thousands. Don't think I'm going to sit quietly by and watch those thousands trickle out of our hands. We've played our first card. It didn't take a trick. Here's another."

Buck and Spalding were leaning forward, interested, attentive. There was that in Emma's vivid, glowing face which did not mean defeat.

"HOOPS, MY DEAR!"

"March fifteenth, at Madison Square Garden, there is to be held the first annual exhibition of the Society for the Promotion of American Styles for American Women. For one hundred years we've taken our fashions as Paris dictated, regardless of whether they outraged our sense of humor or decency or of fitness. This year the American designer is going to have a chance. Am I an American designer, T. A., Billy?"

"Yes!" in chorus.

"Then I shall exhibit that skirt on a live model at the First Annual American Fashion Show next month. Every skirt-buyer in the country will be there. If it takes hold there, it's made—and so are we."

March came, and with it an army of men and women buyers, dependent, for the first time in their business careers, on the ingenuity of the American brain. The keen-eyed legions that had advanced on Europe early, armed with letters of credit—the vast horde that returned each spring and autumn laden with their spoils —hats, gowns, laces, linens, silks, embroideries—were obliged to content themselves with what was to be found in their own camp.

Clever manager that she was, Emma took as much pains with her model as with the skirt itself. She chose a girl whose demure prettiness and quiet charm would enhance the possibilities of the skirt's practicability in the eye of the shrewd buyer. Gertrude, the model, developed a real interest in the success of the petticoat. Emma knew enough about the psychology of crowds to realize how this increased her chances for success.

The much heralded fashion show was to open at one o'clock on the afternoon of March fifteenth. At ten o'clock that morning, there breezed in from Chicago a tall, slim, alert young man, who made straight for the offices of the T. A. Buck Featherloom Petticoat Company, walked into the junior partner's private office, and took that astonished lady in his two strong arms.

"Jock McChesney!" gasped his rumpled mother, emerging from the hug. "I've been hungry for a sight of you!" She was submerged in a second hug. "Come here to the window where I can get a real look at you! Why didn't you wire me? What are you doing away from your own job? How's business?

And why come to-day, of all days, when I can't make a fuss over you?"

Jock McChesney, bright-eyed, clear-skinned, steady of hand, stood up well under the satisfied scrutiny of his adoring mother. He smiled down at her.

"Wanted to surprise you. Here for three reasons—the Abbott Grape-juice advertising contract, you, and Grace. And why can't you make a fuss over me, I'd like to know?"

Emma told him. His keen, quick mind required little in the way of explanation.

"But why didn't you let me in on it sooner?"

"Because, son, nothing explains harder than embryo success. I always prefer to wait until it's grown up and let it do its own explaining."

"But the thing ought to have national advertising," Jock insisted, with the advertising expert's lightning grasp of its possibilities. "What that skirt needs is publicity. Why didn't you let me handle——"

"Yes, I know, dear; but you haven't seen the skirt. It won't do to ram it down their throats. I want to ease it to them first. I want them to get used to it. It failed utterly

[163]

on the road, because it jarred their notion of what a petticoat ought to be. That's due to five years of sheath skirts."

"But suppose—just for the sake of argument —that it doesn't strike them right this afternoon?"

"Then it's gone, that's all. Six months from now, every skirt-factory in the country will be manufacturing a similar garment. People will be ready for it then. I've just tried to cut in ahead of the rest. Perhaps I shouldn't have tried to do it."

Jock hugged her again at that, to the edification of the office windows across the way.

"Gad, you're a wiz, mother! Now listen: I 'phoned Grace when I got in. She's going to meet me here at one. I'll chase over to the office now on this grape-juice thing and come back here in time for lunch. Is T. A. in? I'll look in on him a minute. We'll all lunch together, and then——"

"Can't do it, son. The show opens at one. Gertrude, my model, comes on at three. She's going to have the stage to herself for ten minutes, during which she'll make four changes of costume to demonstrate the usefulness of the skirt for every sort of gown from chiffon to velvet. Come back here at one, if you like. If I'm not here, come over to the show. But— lunch! I'd choke."

At twelve-thirty, there scampered into Emma's office a very white-faced, round-eyed little stock-girl. Emma, deep in a last-minute discussion with Buck, had a premonition of trouble before the girl gasped out her message.

"Oh, Mrs. Buck, Gertie's awful sick!"

"Sick!" echoed Emma and Buck, in duet. Then Emma:

"But she can't be! It's impossible! She was all right a half hour ago." She was hurrying down the hall as she spoke. "Where is she?"

"They've got her on one of the tables in the workroom. She's moaning awful."

Gertie's appendix, with that innate sense of the dramatic so often found in temperamental appendices, had indeed chosen this moment to call attention to itself. Gertie, the demurely pretty and quietly charming, was rolled in a very tight ball on the workroom cutting-table. At one o'clock, she was on her way home in a cab, under the care of a doctor, Miss Kelly, the

[165]

bookkeeper, and Jock, who, coming in gaily at one, had been pressed into service, bewildered but willing.

Three rather tragic figures stared at one another in the junior partner's office. They were Emma, Buck, and Grace Galt, Jock's wife-to-be. Grace Galt, slim, lovely, girlish, was known, at twenty-four, as one of the most expert copy writers in the advertising world. In her clear-headed, capable manner, she tried to suggest a way out of the difficulty now.

"But surely the world's full of girls," she said. "It's late, I know; but any theatrical agency will send a girl over."

"That's just what I tried to avoid," Emma replied. "I wanted to show this skirt on a sweet, pretty, refined sort of girl who looks and acts like a lady. One of those blond show girls would kill it."

Gloom settled down again over the three. Emma broke the silence with a rueful little laugh.

"I think," she said, "that perhaps you're right, T. A., and this is the Lord's way of showing me that the world is not quite ready for this skirt."

"HOOPS, MY DEAR!"

"You're not beaten yet, Emma," Buck assured her vigorously. "How about this new girl—what's her name?—Myrtle. She's one of those thin, limp ones, isn't she? Try her."

"I will," said Emma. "You're right. I'm not beaten yet. I've had to fight for everything worth while in my life. I'm superstitious about it now. When things come easy I'm afraid of them." Then, to the stock-girl, "Annie, tell Myrtle I want to see her."

Silence fell again upon the three. Myrtle, very limp, very thin, very languid indeed, roused them at her entrance. The hopeful look in Emma's eyes faded as she beheld her. Myrtle was so obviously limp, so hopelessly new.

"Annie says you want me to take Gertie's place," drawled Myrtle, striking a magazine-cover attitude.

"I don't know that you are just the—er—type; but perhaps, if you're willing——"

"Of course I didn't come here as a model," said Myrtle, and sagged on the other hip. "But, as a special favor to you I'm willing to try it—at special model's rates."

Emma ran a somewhat frenzied hand through her hair.

"Then, as a special favor to me, will you begin by trying to stand up straight, please? That débutante slouch would kill a queen's coronation costume."

Myrtle straightened, slumped again.

"I can't help it if I am willowy"—listlessly.

"Your hair!" Myrtle's hand went vaguely to her head. "I can't have you wear it that way."

"Why, this is the French roll!" protested Myrtle, offended.

"Then do it in a German bun!" snapped Emma. "Any way but that. Will you walk, please?"

"Walk?"—dully.

"Yes, walk; I want to see how you——"

Myrtle walked across the room. A groan came from Emma.

"I thought so." She took a long breath. "Myrtle, listen: That Australian crawl was necessary when our skirts were so narrow we had to negotiate a curbing before we could take it. But the skirt you're going to demonstrate is wide. Like that! You're practically a free woman in it. Step out! Stride! Swing! Walk!"

[168]

"HOOPS, MY DEAR!"

Myrtle tried it, stumbled, sulked.

Emma, half smiling, half woeful, patted the girl's shoulder.

"Oh, I see; you're wearing a tight one. Well, run in and get into the skirt. Miss Loeb will help you. Then come back here—and quickly, please."

The three looked at each other in silence. It was a silence brimming with eloquent meaning. Each sought encouragement in the eyes of the other—and failed to find it. Failing, they broke into helpless laughter. It proved a safety-valve.

"She may do, Emma—when she has her hair done differently, and if she'll only stand up."

But Emma shook her head.

"T. A., something tells me you're going to have a wonderful chance to say, 'I told you so!' at three o'clock this afternoon."

"You know I wouldn't say it, Emma."

"Yes; I do know it, dear. But what's the difference, if the chance is there?"

Suspense settled down on the little office. Billy Spalding entered, smiling. After five minutes of waiting, even his buoyant spirits sank.

[169]

"Don't you think—if you were to go in and —and sort of help adjust things——" suggested Buck vaguely.

"No; I don't want to prop her up. She'll have to stand alone when she gets there. She'll either do, or not. When she enters that door, I'll know."

When Myrtle entered, wearing the fascinatingly fashioned new model, they all knew. Emma spoke decisively.

"That settles it."

"What's the matter? Don't it look all right?" demanded Myrtle.

"Take it off, Myrtle."

Then, to the others, as Myrtle, sulking, left the room:

"I can stand to see that skirt die if necessary. But I won't help murder it."

"But, Mrs. Buck," protested Spalding, almost tearfully, "you've got to exhibit that skirt. You've got to!"

Emma shook a sorrowing head.

"That wouldn't be an exhibition, Billy. It would be an *exposé*."

Spalding clapped a desperate hand to his bald head.

"If only I had Julian Eltinge's shape, I'd wear it to the show for you myself."

"That's all it needs now," retorted Emma grimly.

Whereupon, Grace Galt spoke up in her clear, decisive voice.

"Wait a minute," she said quietly. "I'm going to wear that skirt at the fashion show."

"You!" cried the three, like a trained trio.

"Why not?" demanded Grace Galt, coolly. Then: "No; don't tell me why not. I won't listen."

But Emma, equally cool, would have none of it.

"It's impossible, dear. You're an angel to want to help me. But you must know it's quite out of the question."

"It's nothing of the kind. This skirt isn't merely a fad. It has a fortune in it. I'm business woman enough to know that. You've got to let me do it. It isn't only for yourself. It's for T. A. and for the future of the firm."

"Do you suppose I'd allow you to stand up before all those people?"

"Why not? I don't know them. They don't know me. I can make them get the idea in that skirt. And I'm going to do it. You don't object to me on the same grounds that you did to Myrtle, do you?"

"You!" burst from the admiring Spalding. "Say, you'd make a red-flannel petticoat look like crêpe de Chine and lace."

"There!" said Grace, triumphant. "That settles it!" And she was off down the hall. They stood a moment in stunned silence. Then:

"But Jock!" protested Emma, following her. "What will Jock say? Grace! Grace dear! I can't let you do it! I can't!"

"Just unhook this for me, will you?" replied Grace Galt sweetly.

At two o'clock, Jock McChesney, returned from his errand of mercy, burst into the office to find mother, step-father, and *fiancée* all flown.

"Where? What?" he demanded of the outer office.

"Fashion show!" chorused the office staff.

"Might have waited for me," Jock said to himself, much injured. And hurled himself into a taxi.

There was a crush of motors and carriages for a block on all sides of Madison Square

Garden. He had to wait for what seemed an interminable time at the box-office. Then he began the task of worming his way through the close-packed throng in the great auditorium. It was a crowd such as the great place had not seen since the palmy days of the horse show. It was a crowd that sparkled and shone in silks and feathers and furs and jewels.

"Jove, if mother has half a chance at this gang!" Jock told himself. "If only she has grabbed some one who can really show that skirt!"

He was swept with the crowd toward a high platform at the extreme end of the auditorium. All about that platform stood hundreds, close packed, faces raised eagerly, the better to see the slight, graceful, girlish figure occupying the center of the stage—a figure strangely familiar to Jock's eyes in spite of its quaintly billowing, ante-bellum garb. She was speaking. Jock, mouth agape, eyes protruding, ears straining, heard, as in a daze, the sweet, clear, charmingly modulated voice:

"The feature of the skirt, ladies and gentlemen, is that it gives a fulness without weight, something which the skirt-maker has never before been able to achieve. This is due to the patent featherboning process invented by Mrs. T. A. Buck, of the T. A. Buck Featherloom Petticoat Company, New York. Note, please, that it has all the advantages of our grandmother's hoop-skirt, but none of its awkward features. It is graceful"—she turned slowly, lightly—"it is bouffant"—she twirled on her toes—"it is practical, serviceable, elegant. It can be made up in any shade, in any material—silk, lace, crêpe de Chine, charmeuse, taffeta. The T. A. Buck Featherloom Petticoat Company is prepared to fill orders for immediate——"

"Well, I'll be darned!" said Jock McChesney aloud. And, again, heedless of the protesting "Sh-sh-sh-sh!" that his neighbors turned upon him, "Well, I'll—be—darned!"

A hand twitched his coat sleeve. He turned, still dazed. His mother, very pink-cheeked, very bright-eyed, pulled him through the throng. As they reached the edge of the crowd, there came a great burst of applause, a buzz of conversation, the turning, shifting, nodding, staccato movements which mean approval in a mass of people.

"What the dickens! How!" stammered Jock. "When—did she—did she——"

Emma, half smiling, half tearful, raised a protesting hand.

"I don't know. Don't ask me, dear. And don't hate me for it. I tried to tell her not to, but she insisted. And, Jock, she's done it, I tell you! She's done it! They love the skirt! Listen to 'em!"

"Don't want to," said Jock. "Lead me to her."

"Angry, dear!"

"Me? No! I'm—I'm proud of her! She hasn't only brains and looks, that little girl; she's got nerve—the real kind! Gee, how did I ever have the gall to ask her to marry me!"

Together they sped toward the door that led to the dressing-rooms. Buck, his fine eyes more luminous than ever as he looked at this wonder-wife of his, met them at the entrance.

"She's waiting for you, Jock," he said, smiling. Jock took the steps in one leap.

"Well, T. A.?" said Emma.

"Well, Emma?" said T. A.

Which burst of eloquence was interrupted abruptly by a short, squat, dark man, who seized Emma's hand in his left and Buck's in his right, and pumped them up and down vigorously. It was that volatile, voluble person known to the skirt trade as Abel I. Fromkin, of the "Fromkin Form-fit Skirt. It Clings!"

"I'm looking everywhere for you!" he panted. Then, his shrewd little eyes narrowing, "You want to talk business?"

"Not here," said Buck abruptly.

"Sure—here," insisted Fromkin. "Say, that's me. When I got a thing on my mind, I like to settle it. How much you take for the rights to that skirt?"

"Take for it!" exclaimed Emma, in the tone a mother would use to one who has suggested taking a beloved child from her.

"Now wait a minute. Don't get mad. You ain't started that skirt right. It should have been advertised. It's too much of a shock. You'll see. They won't buy. They're afraid of it. I'll take it off your hands and push it right, see? I offer you forty thousand for the rights to make that skirt and advertise it as the 'Fromkin Full-flounce Skirt. It Flares!'"

Emma smiled.

"How much?" she asked quizzically.

[176]

Abel I. Fromkin gulped.

"Fifty thousand," he said.

"Fifty thousand," repeated Emma quietly, and looked at Buck. "Thanks, Mr. Fromkin! I know, now, that if it's worth fifty thousand to you to-day as the 'Fromkin Full-flounce Skirt. It Flares!' then it's worth one hundred and fifty thousand to us as the 'T. A. Buck Balloon-Petticoat. It Billows!'"

And it was.

VI

SISTERS UNDER THEIR SKIN

WOMEN who know the joys and sorrows of a pay envelope do not speak of girls who work as Working Girls. Neither do they use the term Laboring Class, as one would speak of a distinct and separate race, like the Ethiopian.

Emma McChesney Buck was no exception to this rule. Her fifteen years of man-size work for a man-size salary in the employ of the T. A. Buck Featherloom Petticoat Company, New York, precluded that. In those days, she had been Mrs. Emma McChesney, known from coast to coast as the most successful traveling saleswoman in the business. It was due to her that no feminine clothes-closet was complete without a Featherloom dangling from one hook. During those fifteen years she had educated her son, Jock McChesney, and made a man of him; she had worked, fought, saved, triumphed, smiled under hardship; and she had acquired a broad and deep knowledge of those fascinating and diversified subjects which we lump carelessly under the heading of Human Nature. She was Mrs. T. A. Buck now, wife of the head of the firm, and partner in the most successful skirt manufactory in the country. But the hard-working, clear-thinking, sane-acting habits of those fifteen years still clung.

Perhaps this explained why every machine-girl in the big, bright shop back of the offices raised adoring eyes when Emma entered the workroom. Italian, German, Hungarian, Russian—they lifted their faces toward this source of love and sympathetic understanding as naturally as a plant turns its leaves toward the sun. They glowed under her praise; they confided to her their troubles; they came to her with their joys—and they copied her clothes.

This last caused her some uneasiness. When Mrs. T. A. Buck wore blue serge, an epidemic of blue serge broke out in the workroom. Did Emma's spring hat flaunt flowers, the elevators, at closing time, looked like gardens abloom. If she appeared on Monday morning in severely tailored white-linen blouse, the shop on Tues-

day was a Boston seminary in its starched prim-
ness.

"It worries me," Emma told her husband-
partner. "I can't help thinking of the story
of the girl and the pet chameleon. What
would happen if I were to forget myself some
day and come down to work in black velvet and
pearls?"

"They'd manage it somehow," Buck assured
her. "I don't know just how; but I'm sure that
twenty-four hours later our shop would look
like a Buckingham drawing-room when the
court is in mourning."

Emma never ceased to marvel at their ingenuity, at their almost uncanny clothes-instinct.
Their cheap skirts hung and fitted with an art
as perfect as that of a Fifty-seventh Street *modiste;* their blouses, in some miraculous way,
were of to-day's style, down to the last detail
of cuff or collar or stitching; their hats were of
the shape that the season demanded, set at the
angle that the season approved, and finished
with just that repression of decoration which is
known as "single trimming." They wore their
clothes with a *chic* that would make the far-
famed Parisian *ouvrière* look dowdy and down

at heel in comparison. Upper Fifth Avenue, during the shopping or tea-hour, has been sung, painted, vaunted, boasted. Its furs and millinery, its eyes and figure, its complexion and ankles have flashed out at us from ten thousand magazine covers, have been adjectived in reams of Sunday-supplement stories. Who will picture Lower Fifth Avenue between five and six, when New York's unsung beauties pour into the streets from a thousand loft-buildings? Theirs is no mere empty pink-and-white prettiness. Poverty can make prettiness almost poignantly lovely, for it works with a scalpel. Your Twenty-sixth Street beauty has a certain wistful appeal that your Forty-sixth Street beauty lacks; her very bravado, too, which falls just short of boldness, adds a final piquant touch. In the face of the girl who works, whether she be a spindle-legged errand-girl or a ten-thousand-a-year foreign buyer, you will find both vivacity and depth of expression. What she loses in softness and bloom she gains in a something that peeps from her eyes, that lurks in the corners of her mouth. Emma never tired of studying them—these girls with their firm, slim throats, their lovely faces, their Oriental eyes,

[181]

and their conscious grace. Often, as she looked, an unaccountable mist of tears would blur her vision.

So that sunny little room whose door was marked "Mrs. Buck" had come to be more than a mere private office for the transaction of business. It was a clearing-house for trouble; it was a shrine, a confessional, and a court of justice. When Carmela Colarossi, her face swollen with weeping, told a story of parental harshness grown unbearable, Emma would put aside business to listen, and six o'clock would find her seated in the dark and smelly Colarossi kitchen, trying, with all her tact and patience and sympathy, to make home life possible again for the flashing-eyed Carmela. When the deft, brown fingers of Otti Markis became clumsy at her machine, and her wage slumped unaccountably from sixteen to six dollars a week, it was in Emma's quiet little office that it became clear why Otti's eyes were shadowed and why Otti's mouth drooped so pathetically. Emma prescribed a love philter made up of common sense, understanding, and world-wisdom. Otti took it, only half comprehending, but sure of its power. In a week, Otti's eyes were shadowless, her lips smiling, her pay-envelope bulging. But it was in Sophy Kumpf that the T. A. Buck Company best exemplified its policy. Sophy Kumpf had come to Buck's thirty years before, slim, pink-cheeked, brownhaired. She was a grandmother now, at forty-six, broad-bosomed, broad-hipped, but still pink of cheek and brown of hair. In those thirty years she had spent just three away from Buck's. She had brought her children into the world; she had fed them and clothed them and sent them to school, had Sophy, and seen them married, and helped them to bring their children into the world in turn. In her round, red, wholesome face shone a great wisdom, much love, and that infinite understanding which is born only of bitter experience. She had come to Buck's when old T. A. was just beginning to make Featherlooms a national institution. She had seen his struggles, his prosperity; she had grieved at his death; she had watched young T. A. take the reins in his unaccustomed hands, and she had gloried in Emma McChesney's rise from office to salesroom, from salesroom to road, from road to private office and recognized authority. Sophy had left her early work far behind. She had her own desk now in the busy workshop, and it was she who allotted the piece-work, marked it in her much-thumbed ledger—that powerful ledger which, at the week's end, decided just how plump or thin each pay-envelope would be. So the shop and office at T. A. Buck's were bound together by many ties of affection and sympathy and loyalty; and these bonds were strongest where, at one end, they touched Emma McChesney Buck, and, at the other, faithful Sophy Kumpf. Each a triumphant example of Woman in Business.

It was at this comfortable stage of Featherloom affairs that the Movement struck the T. A. Buck Company. Emma McChesney Buck had never mingled much in movements. Not that she lacked sympathy with them; she often approved of them, heart and soul. But she had been heard to say that the Movers got on her nerves. Those well-dressed, glib, staccato ladies who spoke with such ease from platforms and whose pictures stared out at one from the woman's page failed, somehow, to convince her. When Emma approved a new movement, it was generally in spite of them, never because of them. She was brazenly unapologetic when she said that she would rather listen to ten minutes of Sophy Kumpf's world-wisdom than to an hour's talk by the most magnetic and silken-clad spellbinder in any cause. For fifteen business years, in the office, on the road, and in the thriving workshop, Emma McChesney had met working women galore. Women in offices, women in stores, women in hotels—chambermaids, clerks, buyers, waitresses, actresses in road companies, women demonstrators, occasional traveling saleswomen, women in factories, scrubwomen, stenographers, models—every grade, type and variety of working woman, trained and untrained. She never missed a chance to talk with them. She never failed to learn from them. She had been one of them, and still was. She was in the position of one who is on the inside, looking out. Those other women urging this cause or that were on the outside, striving to peer in.

The Movement struck T. A. Buck's at eleven o'clock Monday morning. Eleven o'clock Monday morning in the middle of a busy fall season is not a propitious moment for idle chit-chat. The three women who stepped out of the lift at the Buck Company's floor looked

[185]

very much out of place in that hummingly busy establishment and appeared, on the surface, at least, very chit-chatty indeed. So much so, that T. A. Buck, glancing up from the cards which had preceded them, had difficulty in repressing a frown of annoyance. T. A. Buck, during his college-days, and for a lamentably long time after, had been known as "Beau" Buck, because of his faultless clothes and his charming manner. His eyes had something to do with it, too, no doubt. He had lived down the title by sheer force of business ability. No one thought of using the nickname now, though the clothes, the manner, and the eyes were the same. At the entrance of the three women, he had been engrossed in the difficult task of selling a fall line to Mannie Nussbaum, of Portland, Oregon. Mannie was what is known as a temperamental buyer. He couldn't be forced; he couldn't be coaxed; he couldn't be led. But when he liked a line he bought like mad, never cancelled, and T. A. Buck had just got him going. It spoke volumes for his self-control that he could advance toward the waiting three, his manner correct, his expression bland.

"I am Mr. Buck," he said. "Mrs. Buck is very much engaged. I understand your visit has something to do with the girls in the shop. I'm sure our manager will be able to answer any questions——"

The eldest women raised a protesting, white-gloved hand.

"Oh, no—no, indeed! We must see Mrs. Buck." She spoke in the crisp, decisive platform-tones of one who is often addressed as "Madam Chairman."

Buck took a firmer grip on his self-control.

"I'm sorry; Mrs. Buck is in the cutting-room."

"We'll wait," said the lady, brightly. She stepped back a pace. "This is Miss Susan H. Croft"—indicating a rather sparse person of very certain years—"But I need scarcely introduce her."

"Scarcely," murmured Buck, and wondered why.

"This is my daughter, Miss Gladys Orton-Wells."

Buck found himself wondering why this slim, negative creature should have such sad eyes. There came an impatient snort from Mannie

[187]

Nussbaum. Buck waved a hasty hand in the direction of Emma's office.

"If you'll wait there, I'll send in to Mrs. Buck."

The three turned toward Emma's bright little office. Buck scribbled a hasty word on one of the cards.

Emma McChesney Buck was leaning over the great cutting-table, shears in hand. It might almost be said that she sprawled. Her eyes were very bright, and her cheeks were very pink. Across the table stood a designer and two cutters, and they were watching Emma with an intentness as flattering as it was sincere. They were looking not only at cloth but at an idea.

"Get that?" asked Emma crisply, and tapped the pattern spread before her with the point of her shears. "That gives you the fulness without bunching, d'you see?"

"Sure," assented Koritz, head designer; "but when you get it cut you'll find this piece is wasted, ain't it?" He marked out a triangular section of cloth with one expert forefinger.

"No; that works into the ruffle," explained Emma. "Here, I'll cut it. Then you'll see."

[188]

She grasped the shears firmly in her right hand, smoothed the cloth spread before her with a nervous little pat of her left, pushed her bright hair back from her forehead, and prepared to cut. At which critical moment there entered Annie, the errand-girl, with the three bits of white pasteboard.

Emma glanced down at them and waved Annie away.

"Can't see them. Busy."

Annie stood her ground.

"Mr. Buck said you'd see 'em. They're waiting."

Emma picked up one of the cards. On it Buck had scribbled a single word: "Movers."

Mrs. T. A. Buck smiled. A little malicious gleam came into her eyes.

"Show 'em in here, Annie," she commanded, with a wave of the huge shears. "I'll teach 'em to interrupt me when I've got my hands in the bluing-water."

She bent over the table again, measuring with her keen eye. When the three were ushered in a moment later, she looked up briefly and nodded, then bent over the table again. But in that brief moment she had the three marked, indexed and pigeonholed. If one could have looked into that lightning mind of hers, one would have found something like this:

"Hmm! What Ida Tarbell calls 'Restless women.' Money, and always have had it. Those hats were born in one of those exclusive little shops off the Avenue. Rich but somber. They think they're advanced, but they still resent the triumph of the motor-car over the horse. That girl can't call her soul her own. Good eyes, but too sad. He probably didn't suit mother."

What she said was:

"Howdy-do. We're just bringing a new skirt into the world. I thought you might like to be in at the birth."

"How very interesting!" chirped the two older women. The girl said nothing, but a look of anticipation brightened her eyes. It deepened and glowed as Emma McChesney Buck bent to her task and the great jaws of the shears opened and shut on the virgin cloth. Six pairs of eyes followed the fascinating steel before which the cloth rippled and fell away, as water is cleft by the prow of a stanch little boat. Around the curves went the shears, guided by Emma's firm white hands, snipping, slashing, doubling on itself, a very swashbuckler of a shears.

"There!" exclaimed Emma at last, and dropped the shears on the table with a clatter. "Put that together and see whether it makes a skirt or not. Now, ladies!"

The three drew a long breath. It was the sort of sound that comes up from the crowd when a sky-rocket has gone off successfully, with a final shower of stars.

"Do you do that often?" ventured Mrs. Orton-Wells.

"Often enough to keep my hand in," replied Emma, and led the way to her office.

The three followed in silence. They were strangely silent, too, as they seated themselves around Emma Buck's desk. Curiously enough, it was the subdued Miss Orton-Wells who was the first to speak.

"I'll never rest," she said, "until I see that skirt finished and actually ready to wear."

She smiled at Emma. When she did that, you saw that Miss Orton-Wells had her charm. Emma smiled back, and patted the girl's hand just once. At that there came a look into Miss

Orton-Wells' eyes, and you saw that most decidedly she had her charm.

Up spoke Mrs. Orton-Wells.

"Gladys is such an enthusiast! That's really
her reason for being here. Gladys is very much
interested in working girls. In fact, we are all,
as you probably know, intensely interested in
the working woman."

"Thank you!" said Emma McChesney Buck.
"That's very kind. We working women are
very grateful to you."

"We!" exclaimed Mrs. Orton-Wells and
Miss Susan Croft blankly, and in perfect time.

Emma smiled sweetly.

"Surely you'll admit that I'm a working
woman."

Miss Susan H. Croft was not a person to be
trifled with. She elucidated acidly.

"We mean women who work with their
hands."

"By what power do you think those shears
were moved across the cutting-table? We
don't cut our patterns with an ouija-board."

Mrs. Orton-Wells rustled protestingly.
"But, my dear Mrs. Buck, you know, we mean
women of the Laboring Class."

"I'm in this place of business from nine to five, Monday to Saturday, inclusive. If that doesn't make me a member of the laboring class I don't want to belong."

It was here that Mrs. Orton-Wells showed herself a woman not to be trifled with. She moved forward to the edge of her chair, fixed Emma Buck with determined eyes, and swept into midstream, sails spread.

"Don't be frivolous, Mrs. Buck. We are here on a serious errand. It ought to interest you vitally because of the position you occupy in the world of business. We are launching a campaign against the extravagant, ridiculous, and oftentimes indecent dress of the working girl, with especial reference to the girl who works in garment factories. They squander their earnings in costumes absurdly unfitted to their station in life. Our plan is to influence them in the direction of neatness, modesty, and economy in dress. At present each tries to outdo the other in style and variety of costume. Their shoes are high-heeled, cloth-topped, their blouses lacy and collarless, their hats absurd. We propose a costume which shall be neat, becoming, and appropriate. Not exactly a uni-

[193]

form, perhaps, but something with a fixed idea in cut, color, and style. A corps of twelve young ladies belonging to our best families has been chosen to speak to the shop girls at noon meetings on the subject of good taste, health, and morality in women's dress. My daughter Gladys is one of them. In this way, we hope to convince them that simplicity, and practicality, and neatness are the only proper notes in the costume of the working girl. Occupying as you do a position unique in the business world, Mrs. Buck, we expect much from your coöperation with us in this cause."

Emma McChesney Buck had been gazing at Mrs. Orton-Wells with an intentness as flattering as it was unfeigned. But at the close of Mrs. Orton-Wells' speech she was strangely silent. She glanced down at her shoes. Now, Emma McChesney Buck had a weakness for smart shoes which her slim, well-arched foot excused. Hers were what might be called intelligent-looking feet. There was nothing thick, nothing clumsy, nothing awkward about them. And Emma treated them with the consideration they deserved. They were shod now, in a pair of slim, aristocratic, and modish ties above which the grateful eye caught a flashing glimpse of black-silk stocking. Then her eye traveled up her smartly tailored skirt, up the bodice of that well-made and becoming costume until her glance rested on her own shoulder and paused. Then she looked up at Mrs. Orton-Wells. The eyes of Mrs. Orton-Wells, Miss Susan H. Croft, and Miss Gladys Orton-Wells had, by some strange power of magnetism, followed the path of Emma's eyes. They finished just one second behind her, so that when she raised her eyes it was to encounter theirs.

"I have explained," retorted Mrs. Orton-Wells, tartly, in reply to nothing, seemingly, "that our problem is with the factory girl. She represents a distinct and separate class."

Emma McChesney Buck nodded:

"I understand. Our girls are very young— eighteen, twenty, twenty-two. At eighteen, or thereabouts, practical garments haven't the strong appeal that you might think they have."

"They should have," insisted Mrs. Orton-Wells.

"Maybe," said Emma Buck gently. "But to me it seems just as reasonable to argue that an apple tree has no right to wear pink-and-white blossoms in the spring, so long as it is going to bear sober russets in the autumn."

Miss Susan H. Croft rustled indignantly.

"Then you refuse to work with us? You will not consent to Miss Orton-Wells' speaking to the girls in your shop this noon?"

Emma looked at Gladys Orton-Wells. Gladys was wearing black, and black did not become her. It made her creamy skin sallow. Her suit was severely tailored, and her hat was small and harshly outlined, and her hair was drawn back from her face. All this, in spite of the fact that Miss Orton-Wells was of the limp and fragile type, which demands ruffles, fluffiness, flowing lines and *frou-frou*. Emma's glance at the suppressed Gladys was as fleeting as it was keen, but it sufficed to bring her to a decision. She pressed a buzzer at her desk.

"I shall be happy to have Miss Orton-Wells speak to the girls in our shop this noon, and as often as she cares to speak. If she can convince the girls that a—er—fixed idea in cut, color, and style is the thing to be adopted by shop-workers I am perfectly willing that they be convinced."

[196]

Then to Annie, who appeared in answer to the buzzer,

"Will you tell Sophy Kumpf to come here, please?"

Mrs. Orton-Wells beamed. The somber plumes in her correct hat bobbed and dipped to Emma. The austere Miss Susan H. Croft unbent in a nutcracker smile. Only Miss Gladys Orton-Wells remained silent, thoughtful, unenthusiastic. Her eyes were on Emma's face.

A heavy, comfortable step sounded in the hall outside the office door. Emma turned with a smile to the stout, motherly, red-cheeked woman who entered, smoothing her coarse brown hair with work-roughened fingers.

Emma took one of those calloused hands in hers.

"Sophy, we need your advice. This is Mrs. Sophy Kumpf—Mrs. Orton-Wells, Miss Susan H. Croft"—Sophy threw her a keen glance; she knew that name—"and Miss Orton-Wells." Of the four, Sophy was the most at ease.

"Pleased to meet you," said Sophy Kumpf.

The three bowed, but did not commit themselves. Emma, her hand still on Sophy's, elaborated:

[197]

"Sophy Kumpf has been with the T. A. Buck Company for thirty years. She could run this business single-handed, if she had to. She knows any machine in the shop, can cut a pattern, keep books, run the entire plant if necessary. If there's anything about petticoats that Sophy doesn't know, it's because it hasn't been invented yet. Sophy was sixteen when she came to Buck's. I've heard she was the prettiest and best dressed girl in the shop."

"Oh, now, Mrs. Buck!" remonstrated Sophy.

Emma tried to frown as she surveyed Sophy's bright eyes, her rosy cheeks, her broad bosom, her ample hips—all that made Sophy an object to comfort and rest the eye.

"Don't dispute, Sophy. Sophy has educated her children, married them off, and welcomed their children. She thinks that excuses her for having been frivolous and extravagant at sixteen. But we know better, don't we? I'm using you as a horrible example, Sophy."

Sophy turned affably to the listening three.

"Don't let her string you," she said, and winked one knowing eye.

Mrs. Orton-Wells stiffened. Miss Susan H. Croft congealed. But Miss Gladys Orton-

Wells smiled. And then Emma knew she was right.

"Sophy, who's the prettiest girl in our shop? And the best dressed?"

"Lily Bernstein," Sophy made prompt answer.

"Send her in to us, will you? And give her credit for lost time when she comes back to the shop."

Sophy, with a last beamingly good-natured smile, withdrew. Five minutes later, when Lily Bernstein entered the office, Sophy qualified as a judge of beauty. Lily Bernstein was a tiger-lily—all browns and golds and creams, all graciousness and warmth and lovely curves. As she came into the room, Gladys Orton-Wells seemed as bloodless and pale and ineffectual as a white moth beside a gorgeous tawny butter-fly.

Emma presented the girl as formally as she had Sophy Kumpf. And Lily Bernstein smiled upon them, and her teeth were as white and even as one knew they would be before she smiled. Lily had taken off her shop-apron. Her gown was blue serge, cheap in quality, flawless as to cut and fit, and incredibly becoming.

[199]

Above it, her vivid face glowed like a golden rose.

"Lily," said Emma, "Miss Orton-Wells is going to speak to the girls this noon. I thought you might help by telling her whatever she wants to know about the girls' work and all that, and by making her feel at home."

"Well, sure," said Lily, and smiled again her heart-warming smile. "I'd love to."

"Miss Orton-Wells," went on Emma smoothly, "wants to speak to the girls about clothes."

Lily looked again at Miss Orton-Wells, and she did not mean to be cruel. Then she looked quickly at Emma, to detect a possible joke. But Mrs. Buck's face bore no trace of a smile.

"Clothes!" repeated Lily. And a slow red mounted to Gladys Orton-Wells' pale face. When Lily went out Sunday afternoons, she might have passed for a millionaire's daughter if she hadn't been so well dressed.

"Suppose you take Miss Orton-Wells into the shop," suggested Emma, "so that she may have some idea of the size and character of our family before she speaks to it. How long shall you want to speak?"

Miss Orton-Wells started nervously, stammered a little, stopped.

"Oh, ten minutes," said Mrs. Orton-Wells graciously.

"Five," said Gladys, quickly, and followed Lily Bernstein into the workroom.

Mrs. Orton-Wells and Miss Susan H. Croft gazed after them.

"Rather attractive, that girl, in a coarse way," mused Mrs. Orton-Wells. "If only we can teach them to avoid the cheap and tawdry. If only we can train them to appreciate the finer things in life. Of course, their life is peculiar. Their problems are not our problems; their——"

"Their problems are just exactly our problems," interrupted Emma crisply. "They use garlic instead of onion, and they don't bathe as often as we do; but, then, perhaps we wouldn't either, if we hadn't tubs and showers so handy."

In the shop, queer things were happening to Gladys Orton-Wells. At her entrance into the big workroom, one hundred pairs of eyes had lifted, dropped, and, in that one look, condemned her hat, suit, blouse, veil and *tout en-*

[201]

semble. When you are on piece-work you squander very little time gazing at uplift visitors in the wrong kind of clothes.

Gladys Orton-Wells looked about the big, bright workroom. The noonday sun streamed in from a dozen great windows. There seemed, somehow, to be a look of content and capableness about those heads bent so busily over the stitching.

"It looks—pleasant," said Gladys Orton-Wells.

"It ain't bad. Of course it's hard sitting all day. But I'd rather do that than stand from eight to six behind a counter. And there's good money in it."

Gladys Orton-Wells turned wistful eyes on friendly little Lily Bernstein.

"I'd like to earn money," she said. "I'd like to work."

"Well, why don't you?" demanded Lily. "Work's all the style this year. They're all doing it. Look at the Vanderbilts and that Morgan girl, and the whole crowd. These days you can't tell whether the girl at the machine next to you lives in the Bronx or on Fifth Avenue."

"It must be wonderful to earn your own clothes."

"Believe me," laughed Lily Bernstein, "it ain't so wonderful when you've had to do it all your life."

She studied the pale girl before her with brows thoughtfully knit. Lily had met too many uplifters to be in awe of them. Besides, a certain warm-hearted friendliness was hers for every one she met. So, like the child she was, she spoke what was in her mind:

"Say, listen, dearie. I wouldn't wear black if I was you. And that plain stuff—it don't suit you. I'm like that, too. There's some things I can wear and others I look fierce in. I'd like you in one of them big flat hats and a full skirt like you see in the ads, with lots of ribbons and tag ends and bows on it. D'you know what I mean?"

"My mother was a Van Cleve," said Gladys drearily, as though that explained everything. So it might have, to any but a Lily Bernstein.

Lily didn't know what a Van Cleve was, but she sensed it as a drawback.

"Don't you care. Everybody's folks have got something the matter with 'em. Especially when you're a girl. But if I was you, I'd go right ahead and do what I wanted to."

In the doorway at the far end of the shop appeared Emma with her two visitors. Mrs. Orton-Wells stopped and said something to a girl at a machine, and her very posture and smile reeked of an offensive kindliness, a condescending patronage.

Gladys Orton-Wells did a strange thing. She saw her mother coming toward her. She put one hand on Lily Bernstein's arm and she spoke hurriedly and in a little gasping voice.

"Listen! Would you—would you marry a man who hadn't any money to speak of, and no sort of family, if you loved him, even if your mother wouldn't—wouldn't——"

"Would I! Say, you go out to-morrow morning and buy yourself one of them floppy hats and a lace waist over flesh-colored chiffon and get married in it. Don't get it white, with your coloring. Get it kind of cream. You're so grand and thin, this year's things will look lovely on you."

A bell shrilled somewhere in the shop. A hundred machines stopped their whirring. A hundred heads came up with a sigh of relief.

Chairs were pushed back, aprons unbuttoned.

Emma McChesney Buck stepped forward and raised a hand for attention. The noise of a hundred tongues was stilled.

"Girls, Miss Gladys Orton-Wells is going to speak to you for five minutes on the subject of dress. Will you give her your attention, please. The five minutes will be added to your noon hour."

Gladys Orton-Wells looked down at her hands for one terrified moment, then she threw her head up bravely. There was no lack of color in her cheeks now. She stepped to the middle of the room.

"What I have to say won't take five minutes," she said, in her clear, well-bred tones. "You all dress so smartly, and I'm such a dowd, I just want to ask you whether you think I ought to get blue, or that new shade of gray for a traveling-suit."

And the shop, hardened to the eccentricities of noonday speakers, made composed and ready answer:

"Oh, get blue; it's always good."

"Thank you," laughed Gladys Orton-Wells, and was off down the hall and away, with never a backward glance at her gasping and outraged mother.

Emma McChesney Buck took Lily Bernstein's soft cheek between thumb and forefinger and pinched it ever so fondly.

"I knew you'd do it, Judy O'Grady," she said.

"Judy O'Who?"

"O'Grady—a lady famous in history."

"Oh, now, quit your kiddin', Mrs. Buck!" said Lily Bernstein.

VII

AN ÉTUDE FOR EMMA

IF you listen long enough, and earnestly enough, and with ear sufficiently attuned to the music of this sphere there will come to you this reward: The violins and oboes and 'cellos and brasses of humanity which seemed all at variance with each other will unite as one instrument; seeming discords and dissonances will blend into harmony, and the wail and blare and thrum of humanity's orchestra will sound in your ear the sublime melody of that great symphony called Life.

In her sunny little private office on the twelfth floor of the great loft-building that housed the T. A. Buck Company, Emma Mc-Chesney Buck sat listening to the street-sounds that were wafted to her, mellowed by height and distance. The noises, taken separately, were the nerve-racking sounds common to a busy down-town New York cross-street. By

the time they reached the little office on the
twelfth floor, they were softened, mellowed, de-
brutalized, welded into a weird choirlike chant
first high, then low, rising, swelling, dying away,
rising again to a dull roar, with now and then
vast undertones like the rumbling of a cathedral
pipe-organ. Emma knew that the high, clear
tenor note was the shrill cry of the lame
"newsie" at the corner of Sixth Avenue and
Twenty-sixth Street. Those deep, thunderous
bass notes were the combined reverberation of
nearby "L" trains, distant subway and clanging
surface cars. That sharp staccato was a motor-
man clanging his bell of warning. These things
she knew. But she liked, nevertheless, to shut
her eyes for a moment in the midst of her busy
day and listen to the chant of the city as it
came up to her, subdued, softened, strangely
beautified. The sound saddened even while it
filled her with a certain exaltation. We have
no one word for that sensation. The German
(there's a language!) has it—*Weltschmerz.*

As distance softened the harsh sounds to her
ears, so time and experience had given her a
perspective on life itself. She saw it, not as a
series of incidents, pleasant and unpleasant, but

as a great universal scheme too mighty to com-
prehend—a scheme that always worked itself
out in some miraculous way.

She had had a singularly full life, had Emma
McChesney Buck. A life replete with work,
leavened by sorrows, sweetened with happiness.
These ingredients make for tolerance. She
saw, for example, how the capable, modern
staff in the main business office had forged
ahead of old Pop Henderson. Pop Henderson
had been head bookkeeper for years. But the
pen in his trembling hand made queer spidery
marks in the ledgers now, and his figure seven
was very likely to look like a drunken letter
"z." The great bulk of his work was done
by the capable, comely Miss Kelly who could
juggle figures like a Cinquevalli. His shaking,
blue-veined yellow hand was no match for
Miss Kelly's cool, firm fingers. But he stayed
on at Buck's, and no one dreamed of insulting
him with talk of a pension, least of all Emma.
She saw the work-worn pathetic old man not
only as a figure but as a symbol.

Jock McChesney, very young, very handsome, very successful, coming on to New York
from Chicago to be married in June, found

[209]

his mother wrapped in this contemplative calm. Now, Emma McChesney Buck, mother of an about-to-be-married son, was also surprisingly young and astonishingly handsome and highly successful. Jock, in a lucid moment the day before his wedding, took occasion to comment rather resentfully on his mother's attitude.

"It seems to me," he said gloomily, "that for a mother whose only son is about to be handed over to what the writers call the other woman, you're pretty resigned, not to say cheerful."

Emma glanced up at him as he stood there, so tall and straight and altogether good to look at, and the glow of love and pride in her eyes belied the lightness of her words.

"I know it," she said, with mock seriousness, "and it worries me. I can't imagine why I fail to feel those pangs that mothers are supposed to suffer at this time. I ought to rend my garments and beat my breast, but I can't help thinking of what a stunning girl Grace Galt is, and what a brain she has, and how lucky you are to get her. Any girl—with the future that girl had in the advertising field—who'll give up four thousand a year and her independence to marry a man does it for love, let me tell you. If anybody knows you better than your mother, son, I'd hate to know who it is. And if anybody loves you more than your mother—well, we needn't go into that, because it would have to be hypothetical, anyway. You see, Jock, I've loved you so long and so well that I know your faults as well as your virtues; and I love you, not in spite of them but because of them.

"Oh, I don't know," interrupted Jock, with some warmth, "I'm not perfect, but a fellow——"

"Perfect! Jock McChesney, when I think of Grace's feelings when she discovers that you never close a closet door! When I contemplate her emotions on hearing your howl at finding one seed in your orange juice at breakfast! When she learns of your secret and unholy passion for neckties that have a dash of red in 'em, and how you have to be restrained by force from——"

With a simulated roar of rage, Jock McChesney fell upon his mother with a series of bear-hugs that left her flushed, panting, limp, but bright-eyed.

It was to her husband that Emma revealed the real source of her Spartan calm. The wedding was over. There had been a quiet little celebration, after which Jock McChesney had gone West with his very lovely young wife. Emma had kissed her very tenderly, very soberly after the brief ceremony. "Mrs. McChesney," she had said, and her voice shook ever so little; "Mrs. Jock McChesney!" And the new Mrs. McChesney, a most astonishingly intuitive young woman indeed, had understood.

T. A. Buck, being a man, puzzled over it a little. That night, when Emma had reached the kimono and hair-brushing stage, he ventured to speak his wonderment.

"D'you know, Emma, you were about the calmest and most serene mother that I ever did see at a son's wedding. Of course I didn't expect you to have hysterics, or anything like that. I've always said that, when it came to repose and self-control, you could make the German Empress look like a hoyden. But I always thought that, at such times, a mother viewed her new daughter-in-law as a rival, that the very sight of her filled her with a jealous rage like that of a tigress whose cub is taken from her. I must say you were so smiling and urbane that I thought it was almost uncomplimentary to the young couple. You didn't even weep, you unnatural woman!"

Emma, seated before her dressing-table, stopped brushing her hair and sat silent a moment, looking down with unseeing eyes at the brush in her hand.

"I know it, T. A. Would you like to have me tell you why?"

He came over to her then and ran a tender hand down the length of her bright hair. Then he kissed the top of her head. This satisfactory performance he capped by saying:

"I think I know why. It's because the minister hesitated a minute and looked from you to Grace and back again, not knowing which was the bride. The way you looked in that dress, Emma, was enough to reconcile any woman to losing her entire family."

"T. A., you do say the nicest things to me."

"Like 'em, Emma?"

"Like 'em? You know perfectly well that you never can offend me by making me compliments like that. I not only like them; I actually believe them!"

[213]

"That's because I mean them, Emma. Now, out with that reason!"

Emma stood up then and put her hands on his shoulders. But she was not looking at him. She was gazing past him, her eyes dreamy, contemplative.

"I don't know whether I'll be able to explain to you just how I feel about it. I'll probably make a mess of it. But I'll try. You see, dear, it's just this way: Two years ago—a year ago, even—I might have felt just that sensation of personal resentment and loss. But somehow, lately, I've been looking at life through —how shall I put it?—through seven-league glasses. I used to see life in its relation to me and mine. Now I see it in terms of my relation to it. Do you get me? I was the soloist, and the world my orchestral accompaniment. Lately, I've been content just to step back with the other instruments and let my little share go to make up a more perfect whole. In those years, long before I met you, when Jock was all I had in the world, I worked and fought and saved that he might have the proper start, the proper training, and environment. And I did succeed in giving him those things. Well, as I looked

[214]

at him there to-day I saw him, not as my son, my property that was going out of my control into the hands of another woman, but as a link in the great chain that I had helped to forge —a link as strong and sound and perfect as I could make it. I saw him, not as my boy, Jock McChesney, but as a unit. When I am gone I shall still live in him, and he in turn will live in his children. There! I've muddled it—haven't I?—as I said I would. But I think"—And she looked into her husband's glowing eyes.—"No; I'm sure you understand. And when I die, T. A.——"

"You, Emma!" And he held her close, and then held her off to look at her through quizzical, appreciative eyes. "Why, girl, I can't imagine you doing anything so passive."

In the busy year that followed, anyone watching Emma McChesney Buck as she worked and played and constructed, and helped others to work and play and construct, would have agreed with T. A. Buck. She did not seem a woman who was looking at life objectively. As she went about her home in the evening, or the office, the workroom, or the showrooms during the day, adjusting this, arranging that, smoothing out snarls, solving problems of business or household, she was very much alive, very vital, very personal, very electric. In that year there came to her many letters from Jock and Grace—happy letters, all of them, some with an undertone of great seriousness, as is fitting when two people are readjusting their lives. Then, in spring, came the news of the baby. The telegram came to Emma as she sat in her office near the close of a busy day. As she read it and reread it, the slip of paper became a misty yellow with vague lines of blue dancing about on it; then it became a blur of nothing in particular, as Emma's tears fell on it in a little shower of joy and pride and wonder at the eternal miracle.

Then she dried her eyes, mopped the telegram and her lace jabot impartially, went across the hall and opened the door marked "T. A. Buck."

T. A. looked up from his desk, smiled, held out a hand.

"Girl or boy?"

"Girl, of course," said Emma tremulously, "and her name is Emma McChesney."

AN ÉTUDE FOR EMMA

T. A. stood up and put an arm about his wife's shoulders.

"Lean on me, grandma," he said.

"Fiend!" retorted Emma, and reread the telegram happily. She folded it then, with a pensive sigh, "I hope she'll look like Grace. But with Jock's eyes. They were wasted in a man. At any rate, she ought to be a raving, tearing beauty with that father and mother."

"What about her grandmother, when it comes to looks! Yes, and think of the brain she'll have," Buck reminded her excitedly. "Great Scott! With a grandmother who has made the T. A. Buck Featherloom Petticoat a household word, and a mother who was the cleverest woman advertising copy-writer in New York, this young lady ought to be a composite Hetty Green, Madame de Staël, Hypatia, and Emma McChesney Buck. She'll be a lady wizard of finance or a——"

"She'll be nothing of the kind," Emma disputed calmly. "That child will be a throwback. The third generation generally is. With a militant mother and a grandmother such as that child has, she'll just naturally be a clinging vine. She'll be a reversion to type. She'll be the

kind who'll make eyes and wear pale blue and
be crazy about new embroidery-stitches. Just
mark my words, T. A."

Buck had a brilliant idea.

"Why don't you pack a bag and run over to
Chicago for a few days and see this marvel of
the age?"

But Emma shook her head.

"Not now, T. A. Later. Let the delicate
machinery of that new household adjust itself
and begin to run smoothly and sweetly again.
Anyone who might come in now—even Jock's
mother—would be only an outsider."

So she waited very patiently and consider-
ately. There was much to occupy her mind
that spring. Business was unexpectedly and
gratifyingly good. Then, too, one of their pet
dreams was being realized; they were to have
their own house in the country, at Westchester.
Together they had pored over the plans. It
was to be a house of wide, spacious verandas,
of fireplaces, of bookshelves, of great, bright
windows, and white enamel and cheerful chintz.
By the end of May it was finished, furnished,
and complete. At which a surprising thing
happened; and yet, not so surprising. A demon

of restlessness seized Emma McChesney Buck.
It had been a busy, happy winter, filled with
work. Now that it was finished, there came
upon Emma and Buck that unconscious and
quite natural irritation which follows a long
winter spent together by two people, no matter
how much in harmony. Emma pulled herself
up now and then, horrified to find a rasping note
of impatience in her voice. Buck found himself, once or twice, fairly caught in a little
whirlpool of ill temper of his own making.
These conditions they discovered almost sim-
ultaneously. And like the comrades they were,
they talked it over and came to a sensible understanding.

"We're a bit ragged and saw-edged," said
Emma. "We're getting on each other's nerves.
What we need is a vacation from each other.
This morning I found myself on the verge of
snapping at you. At you! Imagine, T. A.!"

Whereupon Buck came forward with his con-
fession.

"It's a couple of late cases of spring fever.
You've been tied to this office all winter. So've
I. We need a change. You've had too much
petticoats, too much husband, too much cutting-

room and sales-room and rush orders and business generally. Too much Featherloom and not enough foolishness." He came over and put a gentle hand on his wife's shoulder, a thing strictly against the rules during business hours. And Emma not only permitted it but reached over and covered his hand with her own. "You're tired, and you're a wee bit nervous; so g'wan," said T. A., ever so gently, and kissed his wife, "g'wan; get out of here!"

And Emma got.

She went, not to the mountains or the seashore but with her face to the west. In her trunks were tiny garments—garments pink-ribboned, blue-ribboned, things embroidered and scalloped and hemstitched and hand-made and lacy. She went looking less grandmotherly than ever in her smart, blue tailor suit, her rakish hat, her quietly correct gloves, and slim shoes and softly becoming jabot. Her husband had got her a compartment, had laden her down with books, magazines, fruit, flowers, candy. Five minutes before the train pulled out, Emma looked about the little room and sighed, even while she smiled.

"You're an extravagant boy, T. A. I look as

if I were equipped for a dash to the pole instead of an eighteen-hour run to Chicago. But I love you for it. I suppose I ought to be ashamed to confess how I like having a whole compartment just for myself. You see, a compartment always will spell luxury to me. There were all those years on the road, you know, when I often considered myself in luck to get an upper on a local of a branch line that threw you around in your berth like a bean in a tin can every time the engineer stopped or started."

Buck looked at his watch, then stooped in farewell. Quite suddenly they did not want to part. They had grown curiously used to each other, these two. Emma found herself clinging to this man with the tender eyes, and Buck held her close, regardless of train-schedules. Emma rushed him to the platform and watched him, wide-eyed, as he swung off the slowly moving train.

"Come on along!" she called, almost tearfully.

Buck looked up at her. At her trim, erect figure, at her clear youthful coloring, at the brightness of her eye.

"If you want to get a reputation for comedy,"

he laughed, "tell somebody on that train that you're going to visit your granddaughter."

Jock met her at the station in Chicago and drove her home in a very dapper and glittering black runabout.

"Grace wanted to come down," he explained, as they sped along, "but they're changing the baby's food or something, and she didn't want to leave. You know those nurses." Emma felt a curious little pang. This was her boy, her baby, talking about his baby and nurses. She had a sense of unreality. He turned to her with shining eyes. "That's a stunning get-up, Blonde. Honestly, you're a wiz, mother. Grace has told all her friends that you're coming, and their mothers are going to call. But, good Lord, you look like my younger sister, on the square you do!"

The apartment reached, it seemed to Emma that she floated across the walk and up the stairs, so eagerly did her heart cry out for a glimpse of this little being who was flesh of her flesh. Grace, a little pale but more beautiful than ever, met them at the door. Her arms went about Emma's neck. Then she stood her handsome mother-in-law off and gazed at her.

AN ÉTUDE FOR EMMA

"You wonder! How lovely you look! Good heavens, are they wearing that kind of hat in New York! And those collars! I haven't seen a thing like 'em here. 'East is east and West is west and——' "

"Where's that child?" demanded Emma McChesney Buck. "Where's my baby?"

"Sh-sh-sh-sh!" came in a sibilant duet from Grace and Jock. "Not now. She's sleeping. We were up with her for three hours last night. It was the new food. She's not used to it yet."

"But, you foolish children, can't I peek at her?"

"Oh, dear, no!" said Grace hastily. "We never go into her room when she's asleep. This is your room, mother dear. And just as soon as she wakes up—this is your bath— you'll want to freshen up. Dear me; who could have hung the baby's little shirt here? The nurse, I suppose. If I don't attend to every little thing——"

Emma took off her hat and smoothed her hair with light, deft fingers. She turned a smiling face toward Jock and Grace standing there in the doorway.

"Now don't bother, dear. If you knew how

I love having that little shirt to look at! And I've such things in my trunk! Wait till you see them."

So she possessed her soul in patience for one hour, two hours. At the end of the second hour, a little wail went up. Grace vanished down the hall. Emma, her heart beating very fast, followed her. A moment later she was bending over a very pink morsel with very blue eyes and she was saying, over and over in a rapture of delightful idiocy:

"Say hello to your gran-muzzer, yes her is! Say, hello, granny!" And her longing arms reached down to take up her namesake.

"Not now!" Grace said hastily. "We never play with her just before feeding-time. We find that it excites her, and that's bad for her digestion."

"Dear me!" marveled Emma. "I don't remember worrying about Jock's digestion when he was two and a half months old!"

It was thus that Emma McChesney Buck, for many years accustomed to leadership, learned to follow humbly and in silence. She had always been the orbit about which her world revolved. Years of brilliant success, of triumphant execution, had not spoiled her, or made her offensively dictatorial. But they had taught her a certain self-confidence; had accustomed her to a degree of deference from others. Now she was the humblest of the satellites revolving about this sun of the household. She learned to tiptoe when small Emma McChesney was sleeping. She learned that the modern mother does not approve of the holding of a child in one's arms, no matter how those arms might be aching to feel the frail weight of the soft, sweet body. She who had brought a child into the world, who had had to train that child alone, had raised him single-handed, had educated him, denied herself for him, made a man of him, now found herself all ignorant of twentieth century child-raising methods. She learned strange things about barley-water and formulæ and units and olive oil, and orange juice and ounces and farina, and bath-thermometers and blue-and-white striped nurses who view grandmothers with a coldly disapproving and pitying eye.

She watched the bathing-process for the first time with wonder as frank as it was unfeigned.

"And I thought I was a modern woman!"

she marveled. "When I used to bathe Jock I
tested the temperature of the water with my elbow; and I know my mother used to test my
bath-water when I was a baby by putting me
into it. She used to say that if I turned blue
she knew the water was too cold, and if I turned
red she knew it was too hot."

"Humph!" snorted the blue-and-white
striped nurse, and rightly.

"Oh, I don't say that your method isn't the
proper one," Emma hastened to say humbly,
and watched Grace scrutinize the bath-ther-
mometer with critical eye.

In the days that followed, there came calling
the mothers of Grace's young-women friends,
as Jock had predicted. Charming elderly wom-
en, most of them, all of them gracious and
friendly with that generous friendliness which
is of the West. But each fell into one of two
classes—the placid, black-silk, rather vague
woman of middle age, whose face has the blank
look of the sheltered woman and who wrinkles
early from sheer lack of sufficient activity or
vital interest in life; and the wiry, well-dressed,
assertive type who talked about her club work
and her charities, her voice always taking the

rising inflection at the end of a sentence, as though addressing a meeting. When they met Emma, it was always with a little startled look of surprise, followed by something that bordered on disapproval. Emma, the keenly observant, watching them, felt vaguely uncomfortable. She tried to be politely interested in what they had to say, but she found her thoughts straying a thousand miles away to the man whom she loved and who loved her, to the big, busy factory with its humming machinery and its capable office staff, to the tasteful, comfortable, spacious house that she had helped to plan; to all the vital absorbing, fascinating and constructive interests with which her busy New York life was filled to overflowing.

So she looked smilingly at the plump, gray-haired ladies who came a-calling in their smart black with the softening lace-effect at the throat, and they looked, smiling politely, too, at this slim, erect, pink-cheeked, bright-eyed woman with the shining golden hair and the firm, smooth skin, and the alert manner; and in their eyes was that distrust which lurks in the eyes of a woman as she looks at another woman of her own age who doesn't show it.

In the weeks of her stay, Emma managed, little by little, to take the place of second mother in the household. She had tact and finesse and cleverness enough even for that herculean feat. Grace's pale cheeks and last year's wardrobe made her firm in her stand.

"Grace," she said, one day, "listen to me: I want you to get some clothes—a lot of them, and foolish ones, all of them. Babies are all very well, but husbands have some slight right to consideration. The clock, for you, is an instrument devised to cut up the day and night into your baby's eating- and sleeping-periods. I want you to get some floppy hats with roses on 'em, and dresses with ruffles and sashes. I'll stay home and guard your child from vandals and ogres. Scat!"

Her stay lengthened to four weeks, five weeks, six. She had the satisfaction of seeing the roses blooming in Grace's cheeks as well as in her hats. She learned to efface her own personality that others might shine who had a better right. And she lost some of her own bright color, a measure of her own buoyancy. In the sixth week she saw, in her mirror, something that caused her to lean forward, to stare for one intent moment, then to shrink back, wide-eyed. A little sunburst, hair-fine but undeniable, was etched delicately about the corners of her eyes. Fifteen minutes later, she had wired New York thus:

Home Friday. Do you still love me? EMMA.

When she left, little Emma McChesney was sleeping, by a curious coincidence, as she had been when Emma arrived, so that she could not have the satisfaction of a last pressure of the lips against the rose-petal cheek. She had to content herself with listening close to the door in the vain hope of catching a last sound of the child's breathing.

She was laden with fruits and flowers and magazines on her departure, as she had been when she left New York. But, somehow, these things did not seem to interest her. After the train had left Chicago's smoky buildings far behind, she sat very still for a long time, her eyes shut. She told herself that she felt and looked very old, very tired, very unlike the Emma Mc-Chesney Buck who had left New York a few weeks before. Then she thought of T. A., and her eyes unclosed and she smiled. By the time the train had reached Cleveland the little lines seemed miraculously to have disappeared, somehow, from about her eyes. When they left the One Hundred and Twenty-fifth Street station she was a creature transformed. And when the train rolled into the great down-town shed, Emma was herself again, bright-eyed, alert, vibrating energy.

There was no searching, no hesitation. Her eyes met his, and his eyes found hers with a quite natural magnetism.

"Oh, T. A., my dear, my dear! I didn't know you were so handsome! And how beautiful New York is! Tell me: Have I grown old? Have I?"

T. A. bundled her into a taxi and gazed at her in some alarm.

"You! Old! What put that nonsense into your head? You're tired, dear. We'll go home, and you'll have a good rest, and a quiet evening——"

"Rest!" echoed Emma, and sat up very straight, her cheeks pink. "Quiet evening! T. A. Buck, listen to me. I've had nothing but rest and quiet evenings for six weeks. I feel a million years old. One more day of being a

[230]

grandmother and I should have died! Do you know what I'm going to do? I'm going to stop at Fifth Avenue this minute and buy a hat that's a thousand times too young for me, and you're going with me to tell me that it isn't. And then you'll take me somewhere to dinner—a place with music and pink shades. And then I want to see a wicked play, preferably with a runway through the center aisle for the chorus. And then I want to go somewhere and dance! Get that, dear? Dance! Tell me, T. A.—tell me the truth: Do you think I'm old, and faded, and wistful and grandmotherly?"

"I think," said T. A. Buck, "that you're the most beautiful, the most wonderful, the most adorable woman in the world, and the more foolish your new hat is and the later we dance the better I'll like it. It has been awful without you, Emma."

Emma closed her eyes and there came from the depths of her heart a great sigh of relief, and comfort and gratification.

"Oh, T. A., my dear, it's all very well to drown your identity in the music of the orchestra, but there's nothing equal to the soul-filling satisfaction that you get in solo work."

The University of Illinois Press
is a founding member of the
Association of American University Presses.

———————————————————————

University of Illinois Press
1325 South Oak Street
Champaign, IL 61820-6903
www.press.uillinois.edu